WRECK

ALSO BY CATHERINE NEWMAN

Sandwich

We All Want Impossible Things

Catastrophic Happiness: Finding Joy in Childhood's Messy Years

Waiting for Birdy: A Year of Frantic Tedium, Improbable Grace, and the Wild Magic of Growing a Family

FOR KIDS

What Can I Say?

How to Be a Person

One Mixed-Up Night

Stitch Camp (with Nicole Blum)

WRECK

A Novel

CATHERINE NEWMAN

An Imprint of HarperCollins*Publishers*

Without limiting the exclusive rights of any author, contributor or the publisher of this publication, any unauthorized use of this publication to train generative artificial intelligence (AI) technologies is expressly prohibited. HarperCollins also exercise their rights under Article 4(3) of the Digital Single Market Directive 2019/790 and expressly reserve this publication from the text and data mining exception.

This is a work of fiction. Names, characters, places, and incidents are products of the author's imagination or are used fictitiously and are not to be construed as real. Any resemblance to actual events, locales, organizations, or persons, living or dead, is entirely coincidental.

WRECK. Copyright © 2025 by Catherine Newman. All rights reserved. Printed in the United States of America. No part of this book may be used or reproduced in any manner whatsoever without written permission except in the case of brief quotations embodied in critical articles and reviews. For information, address HarperCollins Publishers, 195 Broadway, New York, NY 10007. In Europe, HarperCollins Publishers, Macken House, 39/40 Mayor Street Upper, Dublin 1, D01 C9W8, Ireland.

HarperCollins books may be purchased for educational, business, or sales promotional use. For information, please email the Special Markets Department at SPsales@harpercollins.com.

hc.com

FIRST EDITION

Designed by Michele Cameron
Image page 1 © (Santi)/stock.adobe.com

Library of Congress Cataloging-in-Publication Data
Names: Newman, Catherine, author.
Title: Wreck ; a novel / Catherine Newman.
Description: First edition. | New York, NY : Harper, 2025. Identifiers: LCCN 2025007557 | ISBN 9780063453913 (hardcover) | ISBN 9780063453920 (trade paperback) | ISBN 9780063453951 (ebook)
Subjects: LCGFT: Domestic fiction. | Novels.
Classification: LCC PS3614.E6217 W74 2025 | DDC 813/.6—dc23/eng/20250325
LC record available at https://lccn.loc.gov/2025007557

25 26 27 28 29 LBC 5 4 3 2 1

For Michael, Ben, and Birdy, for every reason

What a large target we make.
The great dramas all begin like this:
a surfeit of happiness, a glass-smoothed pond
just begging for a stone.

—Beth Ann Fennelly,
"The Gods Watch Us Through the Window"

Death is a sniper. It strikes people you love, people you like, people you know—it's everywhere. You could be next. But then you turn out not to be. But then again, you could be.

—Nora Ephron,
I Feel Bad About My Neck

The dark grid of the town is punctuated only with streetlamps and garage lights and fireflies, although the bird can sense every living thing: ripples beneath a crisping lawn, a body's rogue cells, the smell of vole, a mother's worried heart beating inside her rib cage. Here's something else it sees: a car moving perpendicular to a moving train, both slicing through the quiet toward the same crossing. The car travels at one speed, the train another, and this great horned owl, perched on the branch of an Eastern white pine a hundred and fifty feet above them, doesn't know algebra—can't predict when car and train will intersect—but if it had hands, it would cover its ears. Because a great screeching has begun.

Chapter 1

In one single day, in two different directions, my life swerves from its path. Even if I don't know it at the time. And even if you might not technically call it *day*, given that it's the middle of the night. There's a headlamp shining out from my forehead like I'm a miner, and what I'm mining is my own insomnia. Like I'm a spelunker, penetrating a deep cave that is filled only and completely with the absence of sleep.

I move my hand to turn a page of the novel I'm reading, and the light catches something on my arm, just below my elbow: a red bump with three smaller red bumps trailing away from it—a kind of dermatological shooting star. The bumps are spherical and shiny. *Pearlescent* is the word that comes to me.

Hey, Nick, what do you think this is? I don't say out loud, because my husband is asleep the way regular people are at 3:38 a.m. Also because I know he wouldn't help me. He'd peer at the bumps and shrug. *Spider bites?* Or he'd say, *Here?* and touch my boob because we are starring in a perpetual middle-aged remake of *Porky's II*. Or, worse, he'd squint at them and say, *I can't see anything. This?* and point to a freckle that is completely unrelated to the likelihood of my imminent death from pearlescent melanoma or whatever the actual fuck this is.

I click off my headlamp and lie in the dark, listening to the late-August crickets sing their song about the night. The trick, as every insomniac knows, is to fall back to sleep before the birds start singing their song about the morning. *Don't google it*, I think to myself—too late, because I am already up and headed for the kitchen, where I leave my phone so I won't look at it in the middle of the night.

"No, no, sillies, not yet," I say to the pussycats, who are busy flinging themselves past me down the stairs, falling down the stairs in front of me, talking all the way down the stairs about their breakfast and how excited they are to eat it. I can only assume that this is how I will break my first hip.

Here's what's true about the Internet: very infrequently do people log on with their good news. *Gosh*, they don't write, *I had this weird rash on my forearm? And it turned out to be completely nothing!* Because after I return to bed, take a picture of the bumps, and plug it into the search engine, and after I wade past the WebMD shallows of bites and mites, I am deep in the Reddit thread r/melahomies, where one person has responded to another, like the world's most perfect bumper sticker, *Just because you're a hypochondriac doesn't mean it's not malignant.*

But what's also true is that this really doesn't look like any of the truly bad skin things. If it's galactic, it's more champagne supernova than, say, dark nebula. If it's cancer, it's more basal cell carcinoma than metastatic melanoma. Suboptimal, sure, but not catastrophic. Knock wood, *kinahora, inshallah*, etc.

Chicken, the older cat, is pleading his case for me to return downstairs and open a can of food. He is standing on my chest and neck, peering around the phone with his massive face, purring encouragingly, and drooling like a Newfoundland. He gives my eyebrow an occasional perfunctory lick. Meanwhile Angie the tabby-striped kitten is asleep again, curled around herself on my pillow like a hibernating chipmunk. I have to stop myself from waking Nick to exclaim with me over the unbearable cuteness of her being.

"Hey, Big Chungus," I whisper-scold the big cat, kissing his whiskery cheeks. "Take a little break from yourself." I turn on my side and he sighs, gives up, curls into the crook of my hip and falls immediately, voluptuously to sleep, snoring like a cartoon human. I am putting my phone away. I am. But I just peek at the local news and there, among the usual headlines about the county fair and the lunch menu at the senior center and a resigning town administrator, is this: "One Dead in Collision between Train, Car." And a flush of goose bumps rises up my arms. The birds are singing.

Chapter 2

I'm on hold with the dermatologist's office and also standing on a stool with a screwdriver in my hand, trying to deal with the broken fan, which makes an occasional revving sound and then clatters around like it's a helicopter about to lift off from the ceiling.

Calls will be answered in the order they are received, a robot is telling me. "In the order *in which* they are received," I say out loud, correctingly, like I'm squinting grimly through my bifocals at a schoolchild I'm about to paddle.

"Honey, honey, no." Nick has come into the kitchen. He reaches up a hand to help me down and unlaces my fingers from the screwdriver. "Let me." He likes to do the man things around the house—the snaking of drains and the splicing of wires and whatnot—and also he has enjoyed more than his fair share of my extreme hormonal impatience. For example, it's not out of the question that I'll Godzilla the entire fan out of the ceiling and throw it to the floor, screaming.

"Hey, do you . . ." he starts to say, and I hold up a finger. "Not urgent, no," I say to the appointments person, who is back on the line and looking at her calendar. She offers me February 7, which is more than five months from now, so I change my mind about the urgency of the rash. There's a cancellation for this coming Friday, and I take it.

"Ugh, why is the floor so slippery and sticky?" This is our daughter, Willa, flopping herself onto the couch in our kitchen. "And ugly."

"Because, my princess angel baby, it's made of ugly tiles and we're too cheap and lazy to replace them and it's humid. Or maybe because we're bad parents. Do you want to put some slippers on? It's hot today. Do you want to wear something that's not that massive hoodie with the hood up?"

"I do not," she says. "But do you want to bring me over some watermelon even though I'm a cranky asshole?"

I do, given that indulgence seems to be the only religion I practice. My dad comes in the kitchen door while I'm cutting the rind off the melon. My mom died a little over a year ago, and he's lived in the in-law apartment behind our house since then. He hasn't given up his rent-controlled apartment in New York—he's just testing this out for now. "Good morning, everybody," he says. He's shaved and showered, as always, and is wearing khaki pants, a clean navy-blue sweatshirt, and New Balance sneakers.

"Do I have to take my sneakers off?" he says, like he does every morning. "I know you people don't like shoes touching your floor."

"You're fine, Dad," I say, like I do every morning.

"I don't know about fine," he says, "but I seem to be still alive, so there's that."

"Good morning, Grandpa." Willa pats the couch next to her, and he shuffles over, lowers himself with an enormous groan.

"Why is this couch so low?" he says, and Willa laughs and says, "We're in the exact same mood today."

"It's freezing out in the shack," he says, and I sigh. It's the only part of the house we've actually renovated, and it's got hardwood floors, pretty molding, and skylights. A waterfall showerhead, quartz countertops, and a view out to the mountain range from every window. The big house is all Formica and textured ceilings—although our kitchen is sunny and glorious, with a glass door out to the yard, a woodstove, and this couch, where everybody congregates day and night.

"Dad, do you want to turn your AC down?" I say.

"It gets very warm back there," he says, and I smile at him.

"I hear how I sound," he says sorrowfully. "Like my own father." He shakes his head before adding, "Doesn't anybody work around here?"

I almost say, "No, Dad, nobody works around here." But then the truth is? We do kind of work abnormally. Nick is a physical therapist and works odd and, if you ask me, excessively discretionary hours. I'm a writer and "work" mostly from bed. Willa works at a lab at the big university in town, dissecting fruit fly brains for money, while she applies to neuroscience PhD programs. Jamie, her older brother, is the only person who has what one might traditionally call a job—he's a junior analyst at Dickens, the kind of massive consulting firm that, say, helps rebrand the flame-retardant chemical company after everyone's pajamas give them cancer and they die—but he lives in New York, and is not here to represent our industriousness as a family.

"It's the weekend, Grandpa," Willa says.

"Ah." He shrugs. "It's all the same to me." Me too, apparently.

"But can someone give me a ride to the lab later? I have to make fly food. Also, I have to euthanize some parents so they don't inbreed with the hatching larvae."

"Ew," I say.

"Coffee?" my dad says.

"Coffee?" I say back to him, and he says, "Thank you. I'd love some."

"I think my coffee invitation maybe got lost in the mail," Willa says, and then, when I pour two mugs, she claps her hands together prayerfully and says, "Iced? Pleeeeease? Lots of half-and-half. Maple syrup. You're the actual best. Dad, please don't electrocute yourself, okay?"

"I disconnected the power supply," Nick says from inside the fan.

"Okay, but don't, like, fall off that stool and break your neck either."

"Wait, do or *don't* fall off the stool?"

"Ha ha ha, it's very funny when somebody has an anxiety disorder," Willa says, and I see Nick turn to look at her—evaluating—before he says, in earnest, "I'll be careful. I promise."

"Dad, when you're done with the fan, can you look at the upstairs toilet? I think something needs to be adjusted or else maybe we just need a new toilet pencil." My dad looks at her questioningly. "You have to poke a pencil into the place where the flusher broke off," Willa explains, and my dad's eyebrows rise, but he makes no comment.

I return to cutting up the melon, and Willa and my dad drink coffee and look at their phones.

"Everybody's videos are suddenly about morgues on cruise ships," Willa announces. "Not my favorite."

"Oh," I say, "I actually had a dream that you and Dad—"

"Ugh!" Willa says. "Why are other people's dreams so boring? Sorry, sorry. Go ahead, Mama."

"Are you holding space for my dream?" I say, and she laughs and says no.

My dad, meanwhile, is trying to remember the name of the plumber in his building in New York. "Do you need something done?" I ask, and he says no, just that it's driving him crazy that he can't remember.

"Shit," Willa says suddenly. "A kid from Jamie's high school class died. Miles Zapf. Oh my god. Mom. His car got hit by a *train*." I look over and her face is a round white tablecloth with saucer eyes and a tiny fringe of dark crew cut.

"I saw that too," I say. Watermelon juice is running off the cutting board onto the counter, and I'm using a sponge to stop it from running onto the floor. "It's so sad, honey. Are you reading the story in the *Gazette*?"

"No, no. People are talking about it online—people from high school. I don't think Jamie was really friends with him, but still. It's so awful. I mean—he's Jamie's age. Was. It feels so close to us." The rims of her eyes turn red then spill over with tears, and she pulls her knees up into her sweatshirt. I bring her the box of tissues and bend down to hug her, squeeze in next to her on the couch and slide an arm behind her. She leans against me and cries a little, blows her nose. "It's so weird," she says. "I mean, not weird—*sad*. But weird too. We *know* him. It could be Jamie or any of his friends." My dad pats her shoulder, his eyebrows pulled worriedly into his forehead. We've kept the worst of it from him—the way Willa's mind can slide into catastrophe—but I know he frets about her well-being. He once asked me if I'd noticed that she seemed *overly sensitive*, and I almost rolled my eyes—it's the same expression I overheard him and my mom using about me, when I was a tearfully anxious teenager myself. "That's not the clinical diagnosis they use these days, but yeah," I said, and then saw that his face was creased with concern. "Don't worry, Dad, we're dealing with it," I said gently, and he said, "Of course you are. I just want everyone to be happy." "Same," I said truthfully.

Willa is showing me the school picture someone has posted. A boy with brown hair and a thin smile. A blue shirt with a collar. A face I don't quite remember but that looks familiar enough. Somebody's child who is no longer alive. "How does a car end up getting hit by a train?" Willa says.

"I'm not sure," I say. Although I have some ideas I don't share.

"That's so sad," Nick says from somewhere above us, his face obscured by a fan blade. "Wasn't he an Ultimate Frisbee player?" he says, and Willa shakes her head.

"Definitely not."

"Was he a theater kid? I feel like I almost remember seeing him in stuff."

"Maybe?" Willa says. "No. I don't think so. Oh, maybe he did tech? He might have done the lighting for *Little Shop* when Jamie was in the pit band. I'm not sure."

"*Little Shop of Horrors*—we went to that," my dad says, surprising us that's he's been both listening and hearing. And remembering too, for that matter. "Grandma didn't care for that scene with the dentist." This is true—she'd stretched her face into a grimace when he'd sung about the joy of inflicting periodontal pain. "Also, where we were sitting—we could hardly see Jamie behind the piano. There was that big light shining right in our eyes." This was almost ten years ago.

"I remember that," I say.

"Let me see him," he says, and Willa hands him her phone. He takes his glasses off to look, then shakes his head. "Awful," he says. "Poor kid. Zapf. Do I know that name?" We don't know.

"I think I played bridge at the rec center with his mother? Is that possible?" He is literally scratching his head. "It's ringing a bell. A dim one. I can't quite remember," he says. "Which I realize is not news. But I think so, yes. Pat Zapf. No, no. Sam? That kind of name. She was my age, though. It must have been his grandmother, I guess. Chris. I think she was a bit of a screwball."

"Like, eccentric?" Willa asks.

"No, no. More like she'd been in and out of psychiatric hospitals."

"Like, she was mentally ill?"

"Yeah. I guess she was more of a *clinical* screwball."

"Girl," Willa scolds him. "No."

My dad shrugs, says, "I am what I am," sips his coffee, spills some down the front of his sweatshirt and curses. Willa blots him with the tissue she's still got balled up in her hand. I stand to get the bowl of watermelon cubes, situate it between them on the couch, and hand them each a fork.

"Was anyone else hurt?" Nick asks. He's standing on the counter now, crouched under the ceiling to screw a pair of lightbulbs back into the fan fixture.

"I don't think so," Willa says. "I'm reading this now. It was just the one car. I don't see anything about the train—like the passengers or anything."

"I think it was a freight train," I say. "So, a driver but no passengers. It was at that horrible railroad crossing in Hampton."

"Ugh—that one where you can't tell where you should even stop because of the traffic light right after? I hate that crossing," Willa says. She's got a mouthful of melon, which she slurps and swallows before adding, "I will literally drive fifteen minutes out of my way to avoid it."

"Smart," my dad says. "Avoiding level crossings—that really is the best way to not get hit by a train."

"I don't know the term *level crossing*," Willa says, and my dad explains that it's just any intersection between tracks and roadway.

"But maybe that's a British term," he says. "I say all these stupid things because Grandma said them." He's talking about my British mother. "Herbs," he says, emphasizing the *H*. "I say sha-LOT like a dingbat, even though regular people say SHALLot. *Gooseflesh* instead of goose bumps. Maybe we just call those railroad crossings. Ack! You again." The kitten has climbed up into his lap, and he strokes her small head with a large, open hand, the way you would pet a dog. She flattens her ears and her eyes turn into happy slits. She has an actual little smile, like a drawing of a cat. "Don't spill my coffee again," my dad says to her and Willa says, "He's gaslighting you, Angie. He spilled it all by himself."

"Rogney!" my dad announces. When nobody says anything, he adds, "The plumber."

"Rogney?" Willa says. "Are you sure it's not *Rodney*?"

"That seems more plausible," my dad says.

"I should call Jamie," I say. "About Miles." Willa shakes her head.

"You don't need to call Jamie," she says gently. "He'll definitely hear about the accident, and he'll call us or text if he wants to talk. I don't think you need to, like, burst into his day and alert him."

I am becoming my own mother. *I'm afraid I've a bit of sad news* was one of her favorite conversation openers.

"REMEMBER THE HEALTH-FOOD STORE ON Ninety-Seventh Street?"

"No."

"Yes, you do. Where we used to buy that granola with the sliced almonds in it."

"The corner store?"

"No! The *health-food* store."

"Wait. Do you mean the Whole Foods on Ninety-Seventh?"

"Of course not! The little health-food store next to the dry cleaners on Columbus—with the bulk nut bins. Where I used to get those lozenges."

"Okay. Yes. Tell me. What? Did it close?"

"No. But the lovely man who owned it—Robby. Or was it Bobby?"

"Oh, sad! He died?"

"No, but he had a dreadful case of shingles, and now he's had some neuropathy in his foot."

I JUST WANT TO CONNECT is what she was probably trying to say to me. Or even, *I'm afraid I'll die—or you will.* I don't know why all our tender feelings have to masquerade as news.

"VOILÀ!" NICK IS SAYING AS he flips a switch. The fan whirs to life and doesn't wobble. We cheer. The motor makes a cracking sound and then a grinding one. Smoke wisps out, the lightbulbs both ping dark, and Nick groans.

"Could I get another cup of coffee, do you think?" my dad says.

And I say, "Of course."

Chapter 3

I'm back at it—on my phone in the night, scrolling through our local Buy Nothing group, where many "gifts" are on offer: a Starbucks card that may or may not have any money left on it, two broken television sets, a dot-matrix printer, a cardboard box full of "pretty nice gravel," a plastic tortoiseshell eyeglasses chain along with a pair of sporks ("Please take all"), a collection of *barely expired* Portuguese spices, a brand-new name-brand twin mattress, and a working air purifier shown with a banana for scale. Also someone is gifting five slices of turkey bacon. *Not our favorite of the breakfast meats*, the poster admits, *but not past its expiration date. Sure!* a game somebody else has commented. *I'm interested. Can you deliver?* Unfortunately, the turkey slices must be picked up in person. I love that people are living outside of the grinding engine of consumerism and exploitation, but used bacon feels like a sad form of resistance.

Don't, I think—but I am already typing "Miles Zapf car train" into the search engine to see what I can see. I'm not sure why this feels so wrong. Maybe because it's a kind of voyeuristic excavation of someone else's tragedy. Heartbreaking, but from a remove because *not us*. Or, at least, *not us right now*. Here's what I find out from a pair of follow-up stories in the news: the train was owned by a freight railroad company called RCX; an investigation is pending, and the interested parties seem to include the National Transportation Safety Board, the Federal Railroad Administration, local police, and, because there was a roadway involved, the highway patrol; no witnesses have come forward; the driver of the train was unharmed and has not released a statement; the family has asked for privacy at this time; nobody from RCX has been available for comment.

I look at a picture of the car, which is flipped over, the driver's side obliterated. I back-arrow quickly away from it. Has his mom looked at that picture? Or worse—did she see it all in person? Did she climb into her own car in her nightgown and rush to her child, where he'd been pronounced dead on impact? The empathy part of my brain shuts down protectively when I try to imagine it—like a gate lowering, and a sign on it says simply: NOT AVAILABLE. No information can be shared between brain and heart at this time.

When Willa and Jamie were little, we played a game called Rivers, Roads, and Rails, which involved laying out illustrated transportation-themed tiles to create a grid of linked highways and byways. And honestly? I never liked the way the train tracks ran so close to the roads and waterways. The kids would be bent over the game with their rosy cheeks, plump limbs, and comically mild oaths ("Drat, I've run out of river.") and I'd be lost to my doomsday imagination: a train sliding from bridge to river one car at a time, like the heavy links of a chain; a car tire stuck on the tracks—like a high-heeled shoe in a subway grate—with ten thousand tons of freight bearing down. I always pictured the kids looking at me trustingly from their seats, me wrapping them in my useless, protective arms. *Let's just agree to walk everywhere!* I had to stop myself from saying aloud. The enormity of my love for these tender, fleshly beings was twinned with a potential for loss so unimaginably deep and powerful that it was like a black hole lurking just outside our window.

Why had we all been taught the expression *Accidents happen?* The presumed inevitability paralyzed me with fear. Was I brave enough to love anybody? Maybe. Maybe not.

There's a handful of comments below the article, mostly of the condolences variety—sorrow, prayers, godspeed, a single *May his memory be for a blessing*—but two stand out: *OMG, but are the shareholders okay?* someone has written. And someone else has written, cryptically, *Accidents do not happen by accident.*

Chapter 4

I'm in my favorite treatment room—the one that's got a poster of different mosses and lichens that somehow evoke skin disease, but obliquely. Prettily. The dermatologist has been studying my bumps with his special black-rimmed magnifying eyeglasses, and now he peers up at me, his eyes distortedly huge like he's a photograph altered by some kind of bug-morphing app.

"I think we're looking at your first skin cancer!" he says. He *exclaims*, I should say. This is literally the most enthusiastic utterance I've ever heard him make. In fact, it may be the first time in two decades he's spoken to me in anything other than a monotone.

"I don't love the word *first* in this context," I say, laughing at him not unfondly. "Also, it's unseemly to be so gleeful about my skin cancer."

"I'm not gleeful," he says.

"You are literally rubbing your hands together."

"Am I?" He stops rubbing his hands together and frowns.

"I killed your joy," I say sadly.

"Well, we're not talking about melanoma. At least I don't think so."

"Yeah," I say. "I googled it. It didn't look like any of the pictures of melanoma."

He wheels his wheelie chair over to his desk and grabs a laminated chart on a clipboard, wheels his chair back over. He points to one pinkly garish photograph, then another. "Probably basal cell. Maybe squamous cell, but I don't think so. We'll likely need to do a Mohs procedure, which is a surgical excision in layers until we get a clean margin." He wheels the clipboard back over to his desk. "This is not a cancer you're likely to die from."

"Good," I say. "My bottom line is being alive. If you have to amputate my forearm or whatever, so be it."

"That's not how a Mohs procedure typically works," he says, and I say, "Yes. I know. I'm just entertaining myself. Can you do it now—the Mohs?"

"Now? No. Of course not. Today we're going to biopsy it. We'll get the results in a week or so and go from there."

His friendly nurse bustles in with a metal tray of metal things and a bottle of something. "He'll numb you up real good," she says and pats me consolingly on the shoulder.

The doctor nods. "It might leave a scar," he says. "The first biopsy I ever did was under my girlfriend's jaw and it left a terrible scar."

"You're a real Chatty Cathy all of a sudden," I say. "I'm not sure that's a story for sharing with your patients, just FYI. I mean disfiguring your girlfriend and all."

"My *ex*-girlfriend," he says. "Did I already say that?"

"You didn't," I say. "But maybe it was implied."

I remind myself that when all the doctors are actual robots and not just humans that act like robots, I will miss him.

"What's this?" he says. He's got a syringe in his hand, and my arm is swabbed and ready, but now he's peering at something on my chin.

"I don't know," I say. "Probably acne."

"Did you pick it?"

"Probably?" I say. He shakes his head.

It's embarrassing enough to have a body erupting in pustules—a body at all, honestly—but it's even worse to have one that you manage poorly. That you treat less like a temple and more like a kiosk selling novelty candy corn at the mall.

"I prescribed you a gel for that. Did it help?"

"Apparently no."

"It should have," he says, and I say, "Sorry."

LET'S JUST NOTE THAT IF a rodeo involved getting diagnosed with rosacea and cystic acne and lichen planus and seborrheic dermatitis? This would not be my first. In my bathroom, there is an actual shoebox—a big one from some Uggs knockoffs—full of all the remedies he's prescribed: white metal tubes of ointments and white plastic tubes of creams and gels and sponge-tipped white bottles of clear liquid. Some have the kind of utilitarian cap that I love—where one side has threads for screwing the tube closed and the other side has a recessed spike for punching it open in the first place. I forget what they're all for, these industrial salves and unguents, so I've started writing on everything with a Sharpie. DANDRUFF or ECZEMA or KERATOSIS, I've written on some. YEAST. TINNEA VERSICOLOR. THE GROSS WART. On others I've written: NECK or EAR or VAG.

"Mom," Willa said to me recently—she was digging around

for something to put on her bug bites while I shaved my leg in the sink—"The warning label on this cream says, 'Not for ophthalmic use.'"

"Okay," I said.

"Yeah, but you wrote 'EYE' on it."

MEANWHILE, I'VE BEEN ANESTHETIZED, SLIVERED, and sealed up with a single stitch and a Band-Aid.

"Praise my bravery," I say, and my doctor looks at me blankly, blinks, hands me the aftercare sheet.

"Keep it covered for twenty-four hours. No showering. No swimming. No sweating."

"No *sweating*?" I say. "Like, I should just—not sweat? Unlikely."

"No excessive sweating," he says. "Don't exercise in the heat. The pathology results will appear in your portal—but wait for my call. Don't look at them and then go berserk online."

"I think you know me better than that," I say, and he almost smiles.

"Schedule a follow-up for one month from now. And get a new referral from your primary care doctor. This one is expired."

"Aye aye, Captain," I say, and he opens the door and makes an actual *get a move on* gesture with his other arm. "I'm going, I'm going," I say. "Sheesh."

"One month from now," the scheduling person out front says. She's tapping on her keyboard.

"I like your fingernails," I say. I am guilty of occasional strategic flattery—but also I like her fingernails. Each one is painted in a gradient from pale blue to almost black, with little moons and planets and stars stuck on, or maybe painted on. Some of them are iridescent.

"Thanks," she says, and smiles up at me, then goes back to typing. "I've got something November twenty-third."

"Hmmm. Isn't that, like, two and a half months from now? Also, I think it's the day before Thanksgiving?"

She shakes her head. "Sorry, Rocky. He's booking pretty far out. Let me see if I've got anything sooner for you." I enjoy the occasional special treatment, it's true. She click-clacks some more on her keyboard and triumphantly offers me November 21. "Do you want to get on his cancellation call list?" she says, and I say sure. But it won't matter. I won't end up back here.

Chapter 5

"Do you think he killed himself?" I whisper to Nick, but he can't hear me, so I say it just a little louder—this is a small town.

We're picking Sungolds at the farm where we've had a community share since the kids were little. Nick is holding the cardboardy green quart container, although he is eating at least twice as many as he drops into it. He's the kind of person who thinks cherry tomatoes taste "like candy" ("Like candy made of raw tomatoes," Jamie always says), but who also really loves actual regular candy, like dark chocolate truffles and banana Laffy Taffy, so he gets a pass.

"Yeah, I've wondered," Nick says. "I think if they suspect suicide, they try not to publish too many details about it—so there aren't as many copycats." There are thousands of suicides involving trains every year: cars on the tracks, people on the tracks. It's heartbreaking to imagine that reading about one would give you an idea.

"But I can't understand how it could have been an accident," I say. "How you wouldn't *hear* that a train was coming,"

"I mean, if he was listening to loud music, I can picture it," Nick says. He straightens up to flip his baseball cap around and wipe his sweating face on the shoulder of the green pesto T-shirt Willa stenciled for his birthday (basil + olive oil + pinenuts + parm + garlic). "Or, like, if he was listening to music with noise-canceling headphones on, he really wouldn't have heard it."

"I guess," I say. I'm trying to picture driving right through the barrier arm into a train.

"Also," Nick adds, like he is reading my mind, "it sounds like maybe the barrier arm didn't deploy properly."

What? This is news to me. I process disasters into two columns: 1) This could happen to us. 2) This couldn't happen to us. There's a secret third column: This could happen to us unless I am very careful/superstitious/grateful, which is the *hubris and why not to have it* column. I can't picture Jamie or Willa driving accidentally into a gate. But if the gate didn't deploy? Then I'm honestly not sure. The child just sitting in their car on the tracks, though, waiting? This is in the third column for me. I pick a tomato that turns out to have a rotten spot around the back, and my finger pokes through into its awful guts.

"That's terrifying," I say.

"Yeah," Nick says. "It's definitely one of the things they're investigating. If the barrier arm didn't deploy, then it's likely that the warning lights at the crossing were also functioning suboptimally." Suboptimally! I love him so much. Plus he's so cute, with his jaw and chin and his dark eyes and silvery stubble. "But it also sounds like there should have been sensors on the train that applied the brakes—like, automatically—when an object on the tracks was detected. So it doesn't seem like Miles could have just been sitting there in his car, waiting for the train to hit him."

"Unless the sensors weren't working," I say.

Nick swats at a bug around his head, and I evaluate my arms to make sure I'm not burning. Is this a bump on my other forearm? A little constellation of them, actually. I peer closer. They could be bites. I can't really tell.

"Yeah, unless the sensors weren't working," Nick echoes. "Though that would be a weird set of coincidences. Or maybe it's all connected. I have no idea."

We stop talking because now a mom and little child are picking too. Oddly, I don't miss this—picking in the heat with the kids. They had to be bribed with popsicles and even then it wasn't quite worth it. I have a memory of Willa weeping because she banged her finger on a green bean. I think we wanted to instill something in them—some kind of value, about food and how it's grown—but instead everyone was just a little miserable. Smug and miserable.

"But when we buy tomatoes from the supermarket . . ." the mom is in the middle of lecturing, just like we used to.

"I'm picking the green ones!" the child announces, wildy.

"Not the green ones," the mom says evenly. She is performing her earth-mother patience for our benefit—or else she is actually just like this. "The *orange* ones. See, Willow? The deep orange ones are the sweetest."

Who names their child Willow? I think—one second before I realize that it is basically the same name as Willa.

"I want to pick the pink and purple ones!" Willow shouts.

"Nature makes amazing colors, doesn't She?" the mom says. "But these fruits are orange."

"Yuck!" Willow shouts. "This one is an orange one with a

crack in it. Yucky. I'm picking the green ones! Green one, green one, green one!"

"You have to leave the green ones to ripen so that everyone in our community can enjoy their fair share," the mom says, and Willow yells, "HA HA HA I'M PICKING ALL THE GREEN ONES!"

She holds one out tauntingly, to show me. "You're picking all the green ones," I say, and her eyes glitter naughty and gold in the sunlight. "Kill me," the mom whispers quietly to me, and I laugh, love her. "That is a perfect child," I say, and mean it.

"DO YOU HAVE TIME TO check on the grapes?" I say to Nick, and he does, so we head to the back of the farmland, where the wild grapevines are tangled up into the edge of the forest behind. A week ago they weren't quite ripe, but now the air is filled with their fruity perfume even as we approach. They smell like bubble gum—specifically like these massive playing-card-sized pieces of grape Bazooka we used to buy after school, but which I can't even find a single trace of online. "If you can't find it online, then, sorry, it's probably a hallucination," Willa said to me once, which may well be true.

"Oh, hello," Nick says, and snaps off a bunch that is so perfectly formed it looks like clip art or an oil painting of a Bacchanalia. The grapes are covered in a frosty bloom that makes them seem paler than they really are; if you polish one on your shirt, the skin will be nearly black. I pop one in my mouth, and the fruit dissolves into a puddle of sweet, musky juice, but the skin is so astringently tart that my tongue feels like it's been sucked dry with a shop vac. I spit out the seeds.

"There's poison ivy all along here," I say. "Be careful, honey, okay?"

"Okay," he says, and then, a bit later, "What the hell is *that*?" I look where he's pointing. "In that maple?" I say. "I don't see it."

"Just some red leaves," Nick says. "It feels a little early is all." Nick loves the summer. I used to think it was about the kids being home from school, but it has endured beyond that stage of our lives. "Summer is your season," I said to him once, and he rattled off a list of things he loved about it: "Swimming, the beach, camping, strawberries, blueberries, watermelon, ice cream, popsicles. Plus my birthday's in July!" "That's a lot of reasons!" I said back to him, laughing, and he said, "One day I'll be an actual grown-up and you'll be sad," and I said, "I seriously doubt you'll ever be an actual grown-up."

We stretch up into the branches to pluck clusters of fruit from their vines, and in five minutes we fill the plastic produce bag I've brought. We head back, admiring the wildflowers: the delicate umbrellas of Queen Anne's Lace and the fading purple clover and the towering spikes of what I think might be called pigweed—but I'm not sure. "I miss my mom," I say, and Nick says, "I know you do, honey." "I don't even know what anything *is*," I say. I could just take a picture, and Google would tell me what I was looking at, but I want my mom. After she got a phone, she surprised us all by using it. I could send her a photograph and say, *Mom, what is this?* and she would write back immediately that it was mallow or bird's-foot trefoil or a serviceberry or oyster mushrooms. *What is this? What is this? Tell me everything!* I wish I'd asked more.

A man with a Yankees cap and an NPR tote bag is hurrying past us out to the tomatoes. He stops short. "What are those?" he says, and I say, "Sungold tomatoes."
"No, that." He's pointing to our bulging bag of fruit.
"Wild grapes," I say. "Concord grapes. They grow at the back there. There's tons, if you want to pick any."
"Are they part of the share?" he says, and I say, "No, not really. They're just growing there along the back."
"Did you ask for permission to pick them?"
"We didn't," I say. "Honestly, there's tons."
He shakes his head in rebuke and huffs away from us. Nick and I chuckle a little unkindly, but I understand the feeling. That there's not enough; that you're not getting what's rightfully yours. Scarcity, even though look at us, my god. We're all as sleek and well-fed as Shetland ponies. What more could we possibly want?

Ten minutes later we're finishing up in the farm shed, filling our basket with wormy corn and gorgeous kale and watermelon radishes and actual watermelon, and he's back. "Maybe other people could gain access to the spaghetti squash?" he says bitterly to someone other than me, and I have to shake my head. If I get another tattoo, it's just going to say that. MAYBE OTHER PEOPLE COULD GAIN ACCESS TO THE SPAGHETTI SQUASH.

"HEY," NICK SAYS TO ME in the car. "Did you hear that Jamie and Maya might be coming up in October?" Jamie's been married to Maya for almost a year, and we adore her.

"I didn't. That's so exciting!" I say. I understand that Jamie doesn't live in our house—hasn't lived in our house, not really, since he left for college seven years ago. But still, the way I miss him feels like an empty room in my body. Like I'm missing one of my vital organs.

"I heard that from Willa," Nick says. He is driving because he always drives, and I'm eating a green pepper like it's an apple. "But I'll text Jamie later and see if they know their plans."

"Yayyyyyyy!" I say. All the kids back under my roof! When I send out my ESP stealth probe in the night to check on everybody, they'll be in their proper beds! I zip my window down to toss the pepper core into the woods. "Yayyyyyyy!" I say again. "I'm so happy." I'm clutching a massive bunch of pink cosmos in one arm, and Nick has to snake his hand through them to get to the gearshift. He glances at the flowers and says, to my great surprise, "Hey, is that more of that rash, honey?"

Chapter 6

The windows are wide open, and there's something almost like moving air coming in. It's subtle—halfway between stillness and a breeze—but it reminds me that fall is not an impossibility. Some of the crickets are making a sustained high-pitched noise, and some are trilling. It's like a movie soundtrack.

"HOW ARE THE CRICKETS SO loud?" Willa asked not too long ago, and we didn't know.
"Maybe because there are a lot of them?" I said.
"How many individual crickets do you think we're hearing?" Jamie said, then put a hand up. "Wait! Wait. Don't say anything. Everybody write down your guess." He was already tearing up little pieces of paper, handing them out. Our answers ranged from six to a thousand. "Do you want to let the mystery be?" Jamie asked. "Or do you want me to look it up?"
We wanted him to look it up—but then none of the search results answered our question. Instead everything was very *Are you hearing crickets? You may have tinnitus!* or *How do you know if you have a cricket infestation?* or *Your first stand-up set bombed? So did Jerry Seinfeld's!* or *Neural Coding of Cricket Sound Frequency: A Study.* ("Ooh, send me that link," Willa said, looking over

Jamie's shoulder.) "In the event, we are going to let the mystery be," Jamie said. "But I bet we're right. I bet it's between six and a thousand."

NOW I SIGH, RISE, CHASE the cats down the stairs, and retrieve my phone. I see the eight jars of grape jelly I've made, sitting darkly on the counter, where I've left them for a gloating few days before I put them away in the pantry. "Guess how much money I spent on this?" I said to Willa last night, gesturing to my jewel-toned Ma Ingalls output. I still had on a purple-splotched apron, and the house smelled like a Jolly Rancher factory. "Zero dollars," Willa said, and I said, deflated, "I mean, there's the sugar—but probably only, like, a dollar twenty altogether." Each jar has a piece of masking tape with just the year written on it. I know what everything is, so there's no need for extravagant identification. "If I get diagnosed with something terminal," I said recently to Nick, "remind me to label all these pickles and salsas and jams properly so that everybody's not just popping jars open willy-nilly in their grief." "Will do," Nick said simply, accustomed as he is to my conversational stylings.

Back upstairs I think to go on Facebook and look at Miles Zapf's profile page. I expect that he won't have posted a great deal—I do understand that Facebook is not the chosen social medium of the young people—or that his settings will keep me from seeing anything much, but this is not the case. Because what I see as I scroll is a robust life inside some kind of specialized arts community. He's tagged in dozens of posts, most of which seem to come out of a group called Melody of Song and Dance, and there are countless pictures of people twirling around each other, Miles in the mix. In some his expression is focused and serious—the way I remember him, if, in fact, I do remember him—and in others he is smiling or even laughing. Or maybe singing. I scroll and scroll, and his whole wall is mostly dancing interspersed with the regular punctuation of birthday greetings over the years. *Happy bday Miles* people have written in the usual way, but I stop at a single *Love you, Milesy!* from a few birthdays back. Chris Zapf. It's his grandmother, the clinical screwball.

I click on her name, and the post right at the very top of her page says, *MILES IS DEAD BECAUSE THEY DIDN'T EVEN CARE ENOUGH TO FIX THE TRAIN'S. THEIR MISTAKE = OUR LOSS.* I note the apostrophized plural, hate myself, scroll down. People have responded to the post with both caring faces and angry faces, and in the comments below it there are heart emojis and broken-heart emojis, and so much sorrow. "Mom, you should probably take this down for now," a *Christine Zapf* has written, and I click on her name. Her profile picture is a photo of Miles with a small dog in his lap, and at the top of her page is a post with information about the memorial service, which is scheduled for the middle of September. In the comments, someone has included a link to a GoFundMe to cover funeral expenses. Someone else has written, *Your beautiful boy.* I seem to have been holding my breath, and I exhale now. This, of course, is Miles's mother.

She has posted a picture of her and Miles in matching candy-cane pajamas, their arms around each other's shoulders, the little dog between them, a Christmas tree twinkling behind. *Always my baby,* Christine has written. My chest feels tight. You have a child, and the child dies, and then you don't have that child anymore. You have photographs and favorite T-shirts and maybe even dedicated brain cells that hold memories of the child. But that's not even how memory works, is it? Your brain, I have been led to understand, is less like a trunk full of treasured souvenirs than like an unsentimental motherboard hosting the careless firing of electrical impulses.

Your heart, though. I once read a story about a saint so holy and devoted that after she died they autopsied her and found that her heart had carved itself into the likeness of Jesus on the cross. Find me a mother whose heart is not carved into the likeness of her children. I put a hand to my own, feel it thumping away like a kick drum, pumping blood all over the place so I can think my terrible thoughts and feel my terrible feelings and get wherever it is I'm trying to go. Which is where, exactly?

Christine and I have a couple of friends in common, I see: one is a teacher from the kids' high school; the other is a massage therapist Nick gets referrals from. My thumb hovers over the ADD FRIEND button, and I can hear Willa say, *Mom! No! Don't!* So I don't. Instead I click on the crowdfunding link, donate an anonymous hundred dollars toward funeral expenses, and hope Nick won't ask me about it—though I'm not sure why I feel so secretive. *She's a person in our community!* I think defensively, not that anyone has asked.

Angie staggers over sleepily and flops down on my arm, and now I can feel her little heart too, vibrating through the top of my hand. She looks like a fox kit, and I am consumed with devotion. It's so stupid to love pets, though! They don't even live very long. Why do we do this to ourselves? "I love the cats so much, I'm basically a furry," I said to Willa recently, and she shook her head, speechless. "You're not," she finally said. "Mom. That's not what a furry is." "Remember how Chicken nursed on my neck mole when he was a kitten?" I said, and she said, "Ew. Yes. Still not a furry."

An email dings in, and I click over to it. It's a new message from the patient portal EarlyGateway, which shows up in my inbox as *ppearlygateway*. Pearly Gateway! Like it's a missive from the afterlife I'll be arriving at ASAP. *You have new test results*, the message says. I hover my finger over the link, sigh, click back over to the Internet. I don't even want to know just yet. It's Schrödinger's rash: Until I look at the results, I simultaneously do and do not have skin cancer. I'll just loiter around scrollingly for a bit.

Maybe I need a hot-chocolate-scented lip balm that comes in a quaint little metal tube? (I can add it directly to the ointments shoebox!) Maybe I need these adorable chunky black pumps, even though the last time I wore actual shoes was a funeral in March. I'm picturing my outfit—black sweater, black skirt, black tights, and—nope. My plantar fasciitis was acting up. I wore my rubber Oofos recovery clogs. Don't need the cute shoes. This lovely lantern on Instagram I maybe need, though! I click on it. It's a frosty white glass cylinder with a curved blond-wood handle. It would be fun to take it camping! I add it to my cart on the website, which is . . . I look at the address bar. Litehose.com. Like *lighthouse*? Or like, *you're being lightly hosed*? "Litehose.com scam," I type into Google, and there isn't anything overly troubling, so I order the lantern.

I learned to check the hard way, after buying a cashmere scarf on a crazy sale from the menopausal women's clothier Eileen Fisher. "That's amazing," my friend Jo had said when I told her. "Their stuff *never* goes on sale." This had given me pause. No, not just pause—a bad feeling. Or really a bad *memory* of some irregularities with the website that I had willfully ignored. Like the way all the images had been the tiniest bit pixelated. I looked at my credit card transaction history to find that I had paid forty-seven dollars to an operation called Eileen Flisher. I tried to email them, but even as I was typing in the address—jjjzhhhhqqqqq123@eileenflisher.com—I knew that I'd been scammed. The credit card canceled the transaction and refunded me, but then six months later a box arrived in the mail from none other than Eileen Flisher! Inside, wrapped in tissue paper, was an inexplicable and asymmetrical tunic made of some kind of polyester canvas. Maybe it's a different category of crime if you at least send *something*? Willa made me try it on, and she will still be teasing me about it on my deathbed—even though we did see a U.S. congresswoman in a press photo who appeared to be wearing the same asymmetrical canvas tunic. "She shops at Eileen Flisher too!" Willa said joyfully.

The cats are draped over Nick's back, everyone snoring softly, and I sigh, click on the results link. *Biopsy by Shave Method on Arm: right medial Antebrachial Region* shows up as a randomly capitalized but clickable link. I click on it. *Pathologic Diagnosis: Granulomatous dermatitis.* I'm no dermatopathologist, but I understand that this is not cancer. I chew a celebratory melatonin gummy and power down my phone. I'll google it tomorrow.

Chapter 7

When the dermatologist calls me, I should be writing. I'm surrounded by my own handwritten notes on scraps of paper, the laptop open beside me on the kitchen couch, a Word document open with the heading, *Spatchcocking 101*. We have eaten more splayed-apart chickens in the last month than I really care to discuss—although discussing them is what I'm literally being paid to do. Every time Willa saw one on the counter, she shuddered, asserted her relief at being a vegetarian, insisted I was a pervert. She and Jamie had pranked me about spatchcocking when they were in high school—they'd explained to me that it was dirty slang for a debased sex act. "A chef's kink" is what they called it, before detailing the associated body parts and utensils. I thought for years that this was true—cringed excitedly every time I heard the term. Even when this piece was assigned to me just last month, I said to the editor at *Taste*, "Should we call it something other than *spatchcocking*? For the obvious reasons?" before remembering that I was a dumbass.

But I'm not writing. Not about the importance of sharp poultry shears, the muscular snipping out of the backbone, or even the making of stock with the trimmings. Nor am I saying, in Chicken's alarmed voice, *Don't spatchcock me, Mom!* Instead I'm mending Willa's jeans. An act of pure devotion. The biggest love in the world funneled into the actual eye of a needle. It's like that Billy Collins poem "The Lanyard"—where his mother gives him actual blood and breath and, in return, he braids her a plastic key ring at camp—but in reverse. *Thank you for being my everything! Here's a patch the size of a tortilla chip on the knee of your favorite pants.* Why so much lanyard, though, back then? I went to one of those horrible urban YMCA summer camps, and we made lanyards every second of every day. Like, we were all in the kind of massively overcrowded urban pool that's lined with drowned bodies, furiously braiding key chains. I didn't even have any keys.

He shows up in my phone as Dr. Strange, for obvious reasons. "Hi," I say, and he says, "Hello, may I please speak with Rachel," like he's an eighth-grade boy in a rugby shirt calling my parents' landline—like in a minute I'll be stretching taut the ten feet of coils so that I can speak to him privately from the coat closet.

"Hello, yes, it's me," I say, and he identifies himself so slowly that I could sob with impatience. "Hi, yeah," I say. "The results came in. I saw."

"Oh, okay," he says. "So you know you don't have skin cancer after all—or at least"—he actually chuckles—"not at the site we biopsied."

I prick my finger with the needle, say, "Fuck," and then, "Sorry. Yes, I saw."

"So that's a positive outcome," he says.

"Yes," I say.

Nobody says anything.

"Well, have a good day," he says abruptly, and I say, "Wait, wait. I mean, it wasn't *nothing*." I see that I have stitched Willa's pants to my own pants and say "Fuck" again, grab the seam ripper to pick out my stitches—though it's funny to imagine Willa walking around with my pajama bottoms hanging off the knee of her jeans, me still in them.

"You looked at the results," he accuses, and I agree that I did.

"I'm not overly concerned about it at this point," he says. "Sometimes we see this kind of inflammation with the introduction of exogenous materials."

"Ah yes! I have been introduced to many exogenous materials," I say, and he sighs audibly.

"It's a kind of foreign body infiltration," he says. "Like a splinter. Dirt in an abrasion."

"It's on the other arm now too, though," I say, "and maybe on one of my shins."

"Oh," he says. "Hm. That gives my explanation less biological plausibility." I am using a glue stick to tack down the corner of the patch before I start stitching it again. I'm always trying to get Willa and Nick to green-light the use of florals and stripes, but they like their jeans to be patched boringly with jeans.

"Do you think I have occult tuberculosis?" I say, and he says, "You googled it! Okay. No. I don't think we need to get ahead of ourselves. I'm going to order some blood work just to rule out a few things. When the results come in, wait for my call." This makes me laugh out loud. "Okay," I say. "I'll wait for your call."

"Well, have a good day," he says again, and I say, "You too."

"THIS IS NOT HELPFUL," I scold the kitten, who bites at the end of my thread and tugs it out of the needle. "You're very naughty. Now everything is spitty and smells like cat food." Willa's at work, so I am forced to do both parts of this conversation myself. "Sorry, Mom," the kitten says, and I say, "That's okay, kitty. It probably looks like a mouse tail to you."

"Are you talking to yourself, honey?" Nick has come into the kitchen without me noticing.

"I'm talking to *Angie*," I say, and he laughs.

"What'd Dr. Strange say?" Nick is pouring Corn Chex into a bowl—the enormous stainless-steel bowl from our stand mixer.

"Honey, I wonder if why you need to eat so much cereal is that it's not really giving your body what it needs," I say—even though I'm the kind of kale-eating person who nonetheless has a massive stable of doctors, everybody whinnying and rearing up on their hind legs and neighing out their copay requests, and he is as healthy as a motherfucking ox.

"Probably!" he says amiably. "I like that this bowl has a handle, though." He pushes Angie gently into my lap to make room on the couch. Now he's crunching so loudly I picture putting my hands over my ears and screaming.

"So? What'd he say?"

"It's not clear," I say. "I think it's basically autoimmune. Like, a rash my body is making for essentially no reason."

"It's coming from *inside the house!*" Nick says, in a horror-movie voice.

"Pretty much," I say. "Which makes sense. I am my own worst enemy, after all."

"True!" he says, and then, "I'm just glad that *I* didn't somehow give it to you."

"Yes, Nick. You are officially not in trouble about my rash."

"Phew!" he says, and wipes pretend sweat from his brow. He is only half-kidding. Or maybe a third kidding.

"Is your dad up?" Nick asks, and I shrug, say I haven't seen him.

"That smells like popcorn," I say, leaning toward Nick's breakfast. "In a good way."

"Bite?" He holds up a spoonful. When Nick feeds me anything, he still opens his own mouth encouragingly, the way he did when Jamie and Willa were babies. It makes me want to cry.

"Oh man, I forgot how good that is," I say. The milk is cold and rich, and the cereal is wet and crunchy and tastes like a cross between Fritos and corn bread. I've been eating lots of raw oats lately, and while they taste not unpleasantly like freshly sawn lumber—or the moist sawdust gathered at the base of it—you wouldn't compare them to anything made at a chip factory. "Thank you," I say.

I finish stitching the patch, move Angie off of my lap onto Nick's, and stand to put the sewing materials away before one of the cats swallows a pin and punctures its esophagus.

"Do you want to go on a little run with me?" Nick says, and I say, "Not really. I have a good excuse, though." I gesture at my notes.

"You can spatchcock me anytime," Nick says—not for the first time—and I smile instead of shaking my head, and bend to kiss him. He stands to lace up his shoes, assures me, when I ask, that he's fine running with a milky ocean of cereal squares sloshing around his stomach, and leaves me to it. I am evidently already overcaffeinated, but I make myself a cup of strong and milky black tea and pick up my laptop. I have good intentions, I do, but instead of writing a bullet list of poultry-subduing dos and don'ts, I go online. I google "granulomatous inflammation skin cancer risk." Because, as it turns out, I have no imagination for a fuller range of medical catastrophe.

Chapter 8

The lab is standing room only, even though I try to game the system by going at the exact right time: not precisely on the hour or the half hour; not directly before people's workdays start; not during everybody's lunch break or right when they've picked their kids up from school. But it doesn't seem to matter all that much. Sure, most people walk around with their blood privately swooshing inside the aquarium tubing of their bodies, but there still seems to be plenty of us who need to siphon some out our elbow hole and show it to everyone.

I sit on the floor with my back against the wall and do all the word puzzles on my phone, send my results competitively to Nick, who texts me various celebratory icons—trophies and ribbons and jazz hands—as well as his own scores, an emoji of two wrestlers, and, when he craps out on the Connections, a GIF of Lucille Ball extravagantly crying.

The waiting room boasts a shelf full of dead houseplants in different-sized pots, their crisp brown fronds and spidery stems withering toward a table covered in dead leaves and also magazines so old that one cover line is "Hello, Mr. President?" over a picture of Senator Barack Obama. There is also an empty water cooler aptly paired with an empty cup dispenser. I feel that this is not the appropriate image to project from a place of alleged healing—negligence and ruin—but who would I complain to? If you aggravate the phlebotomists you end up with a diagnosis of Ebola and rickets, or so I have to assume.

A woman is here with a teenager who is hunched angrily over her phone and also chewing her thumbnail or the skin around it. Another woman is here with a cranky old man in a wheelchair. "Dad," she shushes him. "Dad, stop. They are not trying to kill you. They just want to check your cholesterol." I remind myself to be grateful that I am escorting none other than my own self. What a gift! Just me, with my granulomatous something or other, minding my own business, not trying to vibes-monitor a beloved family member half to death.

When I run out of puzzles, I click over to Instagram. Maya has tagged Jamie in a picture: he's bare-chested and beaming, holding their cat, Angus Beef. I love that he has a cat. When kids willingly re-create parts of their childhood, it feels like such a vote of confidence: cotton sheets, thrift shopping, the good organic olive oil we've always gotten. And then you have to not be offended when they get the other brand of butter or their toilet paper unrolls from the wrong direction or they make smoothies with juice instead of coconut milk.

"It turns out I really like lamb," Jamie said to us the last time we saw him. This utterance was a little more heated than one might expect. "You guys have always been like, *We don't like lamb*. Like, as a family. *We are a people who don't like lamb!*" We were eating burgers at the time (beef, of course—we're not monsters, ha ha), and Jamie chewed thoughtfully, lifted his bun to slather on a little more chipotle mayo. "But then we were at this Greek place? And I ordered the braised lamb shank? And it was so good. It was falling off the bone into shreds, super garlicky and lemony, and it was basically the best thing I ever ate."

"That actually sounds really good," I said, and it actually did. "I'm sorry we kept you from lamb all these years." Jamie laughed. I did too.

"I'm not sorry," Nick said. He was salting the potatoes I'd roasted, which I was trying not to experience as a reproach. "Lamb is objectively disgusting. It tastes like barn."

"Nicky," I said. "Don't. You guys, I really am sorry if we didn't leave you enough room to try things out on your own."

"No, no," Jamie said. "It's just funny. It's weirdly hard to stray at all from the family culture."

"I kind of want to make 'We All Hate Lamb' T-shirts for you guys for Christmas," Nick said.

"Um, okay, but I *do* hate lamb." This was Willa, who was eating a chickpea-quinoa burger that I'd made her. It had tons of cilantro in it, a little bit of feta and ground coriander, and it was crisped in a pan and delicious. "That one is easy for me. But I had a similar thing recently, where I was getting ready to go to a concert—like, leaving ridiculously early the way we always have, and then I realized that I could just get there whenever. Because I don't actually care if I get a good seat!" Willa looked at me and laughed. "Oh my god, Mama, your face. You're shocked!"

"No, no. I mean, kind of? But it's great. I'm glad. I mean, yeah, sit right by the bathroom or with that pole in front of you. Have at it." I laughed, picked a fried almond out of my kale salad, crunched it between my various crumbling molars. "I think it's so good to keep differentiating from your parents," I said. "To figure out what you authentically like."

"Maybe it's not even *differentiating*," Willa said. "Maybe it's not even in relation to you or about you at all. Maybe we're just different."

"Yes," I said. "Totally." *Here I am decentering myself! Look at me!*

"I was thinking recently, like, what if I meet someone who's religious and I want to marry her?" Willa looked at us with a kind of effervescent irritation, and I could see the feisty little girl in her—the one who maintained defiant eye contact with you while she drew a penis on her leg with a Sharpie. "Would you guys just totally lose your minds?"

Chicken jumped up into my lap, as big and heavy as a raccoon, and I stroked his face and neck until he purred. I was picturing Willa with a yarmulke on. Willa in a wimple, a burka, a bishop's headdress. "No, no," I said, somewhat unrealistically. "Of course not."

"I mean, if it mattered to her, I would probably convert," Willa said.

"A bridge too far," Nick said, and everybody laughed.

"We love and trust you guys so much that it's always an occasion to rise to," I said. "The different ways you challenge us to open our minds."

"I'm sorry, but lamb?" Nick said sorrowfully.

"Okay, full disclosure," Jamie said. "I had lamb *again*?

Chops, at this kind of mid bistro in my neighborhood? And they were a little gross."

"We just don't like lamb," Nick said consolingly. "As a family."

I CLICK OVER TO FACEBOOK, and a post from Christine Zapf pops immediately into my feed. Did I *friend* her? Yikes! I seem to have. I make a mental note to be less of a creep. *We would like to be able to simply grieve*, she has written. *But they are making it impossible.* She's linked to a local story about the accident. The freight company has defended both their driver and their safety record, and has asserted that the vast majority of car-train collisions are the fault of the automobile, "intentional or not—and it's a tragedy either way." The article refers to the complicated web of responsibility, and the fact that RCX actually owns the tracks. I'm not sure why this is surprising to me, but it is. Maybe I thought train tracks were just there for everybody to use, the way the sky is for airplanes or the sea for boats. This does not make sense as an assumption, I'm realizing. But trains just feel so benign and uncomplicated. Probably I'm picturing Richard Scarry books: the dog conductor cheerfully collecting the tickets from the pig dad; a raccoon porter getting the pillows and blankets ready for the cat family; Cookie the pig chef flipping pancakes out the window into the dining car. A loyal collective of friendly animals working together to get everybody where they need to go.

I'd do better to picture the game Monopoly: Reading, Pennsylvania, B&O, and Short Line. Nobody is enjoying a dirty martini in the bar or a golden-hour view along the coastline. You're just crushing everyone to death, extracting capital from your assets. Wealth pursued nakedly, with inevitable casualties along the way. "Get killed by a train, go directly to jail."

THE PHLEBOTOMIST IS CALLING TO me from the door to the lab, and I scramble to put my phone away, embarrassed for no particular reason except that this seems to be my natural state. I comment on her new butterfly tattoo, ask about nursing school, which she is loving, prove myself in every way worthy of both love and a good outcome. "Little prick," she warns, which is what a whole bunch of men I know should have on their tombstones. "You're bad," she says, because she is a mind reader. Or maybe I've said it out loud. I watch the vials fill with blood and feel a sense of pride that is truly inexplicable. Maybe I'll add, *Body makes own blood!* to the *Other Skills* section of my résumé.

WHEN JAMIE WAS BORN BY emergency C-section, Nick held it together through everybody's near-death experience until the very end, when they were wringing all the gauze sponges into a bucket to measure blood loss. He dropped briefly to his knees in the OR, reassuring me the whole time, even from the floor, where he was half-blacked-out. "Everything is going great!" he called out cheerfully, his cheek pressed to the cold tiles. I have always loved this story—the contrast of Nick's disequilibrium with his usual collectedness, maybe, or the badassery of my blood loss, or the unspeakable luck of Jamie's first breaths—but we told it to the kids recently, and Willa shook her head. "Why didn't they just count the sponges and weigh everything?" she said, and I said, "What?"

"They could have counted and weighed the soaked sponges, tared for the weight of the dry sponges," she clarified. "Calculated the blood loss that way. It's so perverse—wringing them out. Were they sadists? Vampires? Are you completely sure that's what happened?"

Nick looked at me and shrugged. "I *think* so?" he said. I knew what he meant. We were so panic-stricken and then so immediately, dangerously infatuated. It wouldn't shock me to find out we'd remembered the experience inaccurately.

"I ended up getting a transfusion?" I said, uncertainly, and Willa patted me and said, "I know you did, Mama. That must have been so scary."

"YOU HAVE GOOD VEINS," THE phlebotomist says now, and I say, "I was just going to invite you to praise my veins. They're one of my best features." She laughs, seals me back up with a Lion King Band-Aid, and sends me on my way like she's a school nurse. "The results will come into your patient portal," she says. "But they may be hard to interpret. Wait for your doctor to call."

"Will do!" I say. And it's not the only lie I'll tell today.

Chapter 9

Willa is in the driveway, leaving to tend her fruit flies just as I'm getting home from the lab. Apparently she has to go "throw away" some more parents because they are obstructing her results.

"Tell me about it," I say, picturing my dad, and she laughs, says, "Tell *me* about it," picturing, I suppose, me.

"Take me to Juice Bomb?" she says. "Then drive me to work?"

I'd love to. There's nobody else but me who Willa would speak to in comically entitled imperatives, and nobody else but her whose comically entitled imperatives would charm me. My besottedness with her feels like a gift or an affliction or both.

"Good morning, Grandpa," Willa says to my dad, just as he's emerging from the shack. "Do you want to go get smoothies with us?"

"Do I like a smoothie?" he asks, and I say I'm not sure.

"It might be too sweet for you. Or too acidic. I don't know, Dad. It's like a milkshake but less—"

"Good," Willa says. "But it's still really good."

"I might like to try," my dad says. "Thank you."

"Great," I say. "Do you need to get ready?"

My dad looks down at himself, looks back up, and shrugs. "I have shoes on. And pants."

I laugh. "Perfect!" I say, and we pile into the car, my dad sitting down in the passenger seat with a big groan. "Why are you standing there?" he says to me, offended, because I'm waiting to shut the door after him, and I say, "No reason," and nudge the door slightly toward him with my foot before walking around to my side.

Have you ever taken an elderly parent to a juice bar? No? Don't start now.

The line is long, and my dad squints at the menu behind the counter. "Is pitaya just a different spelling of *papaya*?" he asks. It's not. "So what's pitaya, then?" I don't actually know. *What is collagen? Ashwagandha? Wheatgrass?* "Are maca and matcha the same thing?" I say I don't think so. "Is *cacko* just cocoa?" Cuh-COW. And yes. "Why do they spell it like that?" He's seen it in the crossword puzzle before, but not in real life. "Are cuh-COW *nibs* like chocolate chips?" Not as much as you might hope. *What is goji? What is spirulina?* Because he doesn't hear well, we're shouting at him, and I can hear how abusive it sounds—like we're bullying an old man with a verbal catalogue of superfoods.

"Dad," I finally say. "Maybe don't focus on all the nutritional add-ins. It's more like, do you want something that tastes like peanut butter? Or do you want something that tastes like fruit?"

"Don't rush me, Rachel," he says. "I'm just seeing what there is. Willa, am I going to make you late, though?"

"Not at all," my daughter says graciously. "We'd be in this line with or without you. Take your time, Grandpa."

"Do you want to sit, Dad?" I say. "I can bring the menu up on my phone." He shakes his head impatiently.

"What's bee pollen?" he asks, then adds, "I mean, I know what bee pollen is. Just not in this context. What's uh-KAI?"

"It's actually pronounced *ah-sa-EE*," Willa says. "It's a kind of berry. It's very purple and yummy. That's what I'm getting."

"Why does it have to be in a bowl? Why just that one is in a bowl, and the rest are in cups?"

I'm picturing Willa and Jamie as preschoolers, unspooling their endless, looping chain of questions. *Why I can look but not touch? Why it's fragile? Why it's made of glass? Why glass is made of sand? Why the sand melts? Why because it gets very very hot?* It always ended with a stumper, like something about transparency, and you'd find yourself backed into a bewildering disquisition on amorphous solids. A friend of ours is a physicist, and we used to keep a running list of questions for him. "Why can't you see stars during the day?" we'd ask over dinner. "How many molecules of ink are in a single dot of Magic Marker?" "Why is glass clear?"

"I've wondered that too," Willa says to my dad, about the acai bowls. "It's just the way they do it. It's a little thicker than a regular smoothie—kind of like sorbet—and then they put stuff on it. Granola and coconut. The cacao nibs."

"Hm," my dad says. "I think I'm going to get that pineapple and passion fruit drink. The Brazilian Queen."

"Are you sure you like passion fruit?" I say, and my dad says,

"I guess we'll find out, Rachel. If I don't like it, I will throw it away. The stakes are really quite low." This is an inarguably good point. "What *liquid of my choosing* do I want?" The line is moving forward and Willa puts a gentle hand to his back to encourage him that direction. The space is filled with reggae, specifically Ziggy Marley singing his own father's soothing "One Love."

"Juice?" I say. "Milk?" My dad reads aloud from the menu, "Oat milk? Hemp milk? *Pea* milk? Maybe not pea milk."

"*Milk* milk?" I say, and he frowns.

"I don't think so," he says. "I think coconut milk is what I want."

At the cash register my father answers all the juicer's questions thoughtfully and surprises us by adding *power greens* to his order. "That's spinach and kale," I say. "Blended into your drink."

"Yes," he says. "I am able to read." Willa catches my eye, makes a *yikes* face.

"I'm actually getting the exact same thing as him," I'm forced to admit, and my dad laughs with true mirth. When the cashier announces the absurd total, I hand over a credit card while my dad performs his shock and horror and mentions cashing out the rest of his IRA.

We sit at a table to wait for our drinks and admire the burstingly gorgeous college students, who are all the same gender, and that gender is mullet haircut, small mustache, pearl choker, ribbed crop top. A year ago, when he first came to live with us after my mom died, my dad would have had something to say about these inscrutable kids, but he doesn't now. He adores our un-girly Willa and her queer friends. He is growing and changing like the rest of us.

The plants here are so lush that the whole place feels like a jungle: dark, shiny leaves everywhere; fountaining green spider plants; vines stretching across the ceiling and down the walls. It's tropical and overheated. I forget to think twice and peel my sweatshirt off, and the worrywarts are on me in a flash. "Why are you covered in bandages?" my dad says, gesturing at the blood-work elbow and the biopsy forearm.

"Jesus, Mom!" Willa says. "What happened to you?"

"You guys," I say. "It's two Band-Aids. It's not like my head is wrapped in gauze."

"Okay," Willa says. "But what is it and why is it a secret?"

"Not a secret. Routine blood work," I say, pointing to the elbow. I point to the forearm: "And tiny biopsy."

"Dr. Scalpelhands?" Willa says, which is our other nickname for Dr. Strange, and I nod. "Mole?" my dad asks, and I say, "Mole."

"What?" he says.

"Mole!" I say and he looks at me blankly. "Mole! Yes! MOLE!"

"I heard you the first time," he says irritably, and our smoothies arrive.

My dad sips tentatively through the straw, shakes his head. "Marvelous," he muses. "Absolutely delicious."

"Slay," Willa says. "Look at you go, Grandpa!"

"I wasn't sure I'd like it, but I love it." My dad sips again. "Grandma would have loved this too," he says to Willa. "She was into health food before it was even a fad."

"What kinds of things?" Willa asks. She's using her spoon to scrape decorative tunnels and roadways into her acai bowl, eating all the crunchy toppings first.

"Healthy things," my dad says. "I don't know. She put wood chips in all our food for a while. And dirt." Willa raises her eyebrows questioningly, and I say, "I think it was very coarse bran, not wood chips. She really did put it in everything. Like, it was in the muesli, the bread, the meat loaf. I'm not sure about the dirt, though."

"It wasn't dirt," my dad clarifies. "But it tasted like dirt. You know what I mean, Rocky. The thing that was like chocolate, but dusty. Greasy. Dessert but not really."

"Carob," I say, and he says, "Carob! Yes. You don't hear so much about carob anymore." This is true. It's all cacao now.

"Grandma and I did eat a pot brownie once," my dad says. "A *carob* pot brownie, of all things. At a party."

Willa laughs. "Do tell!"

"I didn't feel any different," my dad says. He takes a delicate sip through his straw. "But Grandma laughed her head off—I don't remember what was so funny; maybe nothing was—and then she fell asleep on the couch, out in the living room, where there was music and people dancing."

"She was so real for that," Willa says.

"I can't believe I've never heard that story before," I say, and suddenly I miss my mom so much it's like I'm swimming too quickly to the surface, bubbles of oxygen exploding in my heart, my brain. The bends, but grief: her voice, her face, the beach-rose smell of her hair, how much she loved us. Willa the world-class empath wraps her arm around me and says, "I'm sorry, Mama," and I shake my head, tip it back to keep the tears from spilling over.

"Don't cry or I'll cry," my dad says. He has not historically been a crier, but he is one now, because that's how life is. You don't yet know who you'll become.

But now he's taken out his famous Altoids tin, and he digs around in the mints and hearing-aid batteries and prescription capsules and tablets.

"Are you about to offer me half a Valium?" I say, and he shakes his head, presses his chin toward his sternum, and says simply, "Heartburn."

Chapter 10

It's nighttime, a million degrees in summer's last flash of heat, and I'm in a T-shirt and underpants, lying on the bed with a laptop balanced on my thighs, reading an email from an editor I've never worked with. Next to me, Nick is watching a YouTube video on his phone about how to rewire the ceiling fan.

"I feel like you're actually *not* 'familiar with wiring safety,'" I say, quoting from the video, and he says, "I actually am."

"The guy just said to leave a note on the breaker box after you turn the power off—so that nobody turns it back on while you're working and electrocutes you," I say. "You have literally never done that."

"I think the risk of you suddenly learning where the breaker box is and doing something to it is pretty low." That's fair.

"Please, can you just call an electrician?" I say, and Nick says, "If you're very nice to me," and rolls over to slide a hand under my T-shirt.

"Ew, Dad, hello. I'm still here." Willa is on my other side, entering fly data into a graphing app.

"Sorry, honey," Nick says, and rolls back over to finish learning how to poke a screwdriver into a live socket and die.

The editor is responding to my pitch about finding meaning

in small moments—bringing soup to an older neighbor, grooming a pet, looking up at the stars—and he's being kind of a dick about it. "Can I just read this to you guys?" I say. "Okay, this is all in block caps, after he's agreed to assign me the piece: 'NO BE HERE NOW. NO LIVE IN THE MOMENT. NO ZEN VIBE PLEASE.'"

"But 'be here now' is your whole brand!" Willa says. "Maybe he's never read any of your stuff. Or maybe he *has*."

"Maybe he has," I say sadly.

"Bro," she says to me. "Ugh. Why are men such relentless turds? He's probably my age. And I'm sorry—is he mansplaining *essay writing* to you?"

"I literally wrote the essay on how to write an essay!" I say, and she laughs, says, "You literally did!" (It's called "How to Write an Essay: An Essay on Essay Writing," and it's on LitPub.)

I respond to his email. *Don't worry!* I write. *The whole piece is going to be very HOW TO JUST GO AHEAD AND BE A TOTAL DOUCHE BECAUSE WHY NOT WHO EVEN FUCKING CARES.* I save this as a draft, close my laptop.

Willa has stopped working and is now watching various vegetarian-themed videos about animals and food. "Our first clue that we shouldn't be eating veal?" she says. "It's the word *veal*. I mean, please. And another question I have?"

"Yes?" I say.

"It's about prune juice. They dry the plums and then—what? Add water to them so they can eke out some juice? That makes literally zero sense. Why not just juice the plums?" I don't know. "And don't call prunes fruit, please," she adds irritably. "Berries and melons are fruit. Prunes—no."

"Noted," I say.

"Mom, are you even listening to me? It honestly looks like you're one hundred percent occupied with picking croissant flakes off of your chest and eating them."

"I shouldn't have brought this huge pastry into bed," I admit. "It's pretty distracting."

I see that my blood work results have arrived in the portal.

"It's from the Latin *vitellus*," Nick says. "*Veal* is. Which, aptly enough, means *calf*." You really never know what Nick will turn out to know—or when he will think to mention it.

"Okay, Homer," Willa says to him, and I can feel Nick decide not to tell her that Homer wrote in Greek, not Latin. He's watching the end of a Red Sox game now, with the sound off, and Willa says, "Oh my god—they still play baseball? That's so quaint!" She puts her phone on the bedside table and rolls over to drape a hot arm over my hot torso. She was like this as a baby too—always scooching closer, closer, closer, until she was pressed up against you, zipped into her pajamas like a summer sausage in its casing, everybody sweltering and delirious with love.

"Aren't you going out?" I say, and she says, "I'm supposed to? But I might cancel. It feels like it's a million o'clock, and I kind of just want to rot here. Oooh, let's turn the AC on so I can get under the covers and be cozy!"

"Of course, honey," Nick says. "Since you hate planet Earth so much, let's destroy it."

"Sigh," Willa says. She sits up, bends over to drag Chicken

from the foot of the bed. He lies on his back between us, blinking lovingly out of his upside-down face and kneading the air with his massive tiger paws. Angie leaps lightly onto the mattress and tunnels under the sheet to make a tight lump the size and shape of a purring dinner roll. Willa pats the lump, tells it what a good girl it is.

"Mom, are you obsessed with the Miles Zapf story?"

"Yes," I say.

"Me too," she says.

"Because it feels like an accident that could happen to anybody?" I ask.

WILLA AND I BOTH HAVE a diagnosis of generalized anxiety disorder, which we take medication for, and which is harrowing at times. If, by *harrowing*, I mean nearly unsurvivable. Brains look so robustly meaty in photographs, don't they? All of that rubbery pink tubing, like your skull is filled with hot dogs. But mental health is as fragile as a soufflé. When Willa was a miserable teenager, I experienced an almost supernatural kind of empathy. I felt it myself, her panic and unhappiness, like it was a duet of suffering. "This is so pointless," I used to say to Nick. "It's not helpful to her that I'm unhappy too." But I was wrong. "You carried some of it for me, Mama," Willa said recently, when we were reflecting on those hard years. "You carried some of it, and because of that, I could lay some of it down." I cried then. That's the dream, of course—that your care relieves a burden from your beloveds. I picture it so literally: helping Willa out of her massive backpack of trouble and sliding it onto my own shoulders to walk beside her.

"KIND OF BECAUSE IT COULD happen to anyone," she answers. "Also because we kind of knew him? Or maybe because we kind of *didn't* know him, even though we could have."

"I really understand that." I've put the remains of the croissant on the bedside table, and now I'm stroking Willa's bristly crew cut and getting away with it.

"It seems like there's this question still about whether he wanted to get hit by the train, which is so sad to imagine. I mean, obviously."

"I know." I'm trying to say as little as possible so I don't accidentally amplify her anxiety or introduce some other thing she hadn't even thought to fret about.

"Also?" she says. "I read something weird—about how the railroad company maybe didn't update their safety equipment. On the trains or maybe on the tracks. It might have been both." I haven't seen this. I don't share that I'm mostly just grief-stalking the family.

"Who's in charge of figuring that out?" I say, and she says she's not sure.

It's getting dark now, and when I turn my head to look at her face, I can't really see it. I can feel her mood, though: melancholy, afraid, grateful. Or maybe I'm just projecting.

I FILL MY LUNGS WITH the fragrance of Willa's musky hair, of her green-apple seltzer fizzing on the bedside table, of Chicken's cat-food breath, of Nick's hot body next to mine. The late-summer crickets are singing together and alone: chirped chords and high-pitched, trilling solos. An owl hoots from the woods behind our house, and Chicken's ears swivel toward the sound. Willa reassures him that he can neither eat the owl nor get eaten by it, so he should just relax and be her baby. There is still a stripe of light at the bottom of the sky, above the mountain range we can see from our bedroom window. Maybe Miles Zapf's mom is looking at the light too, from the other side of our town. Maybe she feels peaceful. Or resolved. Or maybe sorrow has turned her completely inside out, her heart beating forever on the outside of her body until it stops. I really don't know anything.

Chapter 11

Willa has roused herself to meet her friends at the bubble-tea place, so it's just me and Nick now. "What do you want to do?" he says, pushing a hand beneath me to grope my ass. "Netflix and chill?" He looks at my phone to see what I'm looking at and says, "Or we could just scroll around in your patient portal. Also fun."

There are lots and lots of results, and I don't know what they all are or mean—and most of them seem fine. Everything in the lipid panel falls into the normal range. The syphilis antibody screen is negative—phew, right?—as is the T-SPOT.TB test, so I will not be going to a sanitorium for consumptives. The comprehensive metabolic panel looks mostly normal—the BUN and chloride and albumin and whatever all else—except for "total protein," which is a little high. Something called the C-reactive protein is very high. But the LFTs hepatic panel looks mostly good, though two of the liver enzymes are slightly elevated. Creatinine sounds too much like *cretin*, so I'm glad it's low.

"How's it all looking?" Nick says. "Great so far!" I lie. "I have the *anion gap* of a teenager."

The CBC panel I recognize from watching years of the TV

show *ER*. "CBC, lytes, chem 7! On my count, people!" Nick still yells out if I complain about a minor ache or pain—and these results are mixed. Absolute monos are a little high; neuts and absolute lymphs are a little low. I seem to have a normal amount of red blood cells, which I've at least heard of, and immature granulocytes, which I have not. My white blood cell count is below the target range. Okay.

One stand-alone result is completely inscrutable to me. It's something called ANA, and the value is 1:10240. I google it and read, *Antinuclear antibody (ANA) test results are typically reported as a titer. The titer is reported as a ratio, such as 1:40, 1:80, 1:160.* I know what a titer is from Willa: it's a way they measure how concentrated a substance is in a solution by seeing how much they can dilute the solution and still find the substance. I guess that they diluted my blood—what? By a factor of ten thousand? This doesn't seem ideal. *We put a tiny droplet of your blood in the ocean, and there were still antinuclear antibodies.* I should dig out my NO NUKES T-shirt from the 1980s.

The Google AI summary wants me to understand a few things about the ANA tests: that antinuclear antibodies attack healthy cells instead of foreign substances (sigh) and that test results can help diagnose autoimmune disorders such as lupus and rheumatoid arthritis. "A positive ANA in someone who also has joint pain may suggest an underlying condition that causes joint problems," the bot concludes.

"You don't have joint pain, do you?" Nick is apparently still reading over my shoulder.

"I don't know," I say. I straighten my legs and flex my ankles. We hear approximately a trillion popping sounds, and I see a new patch of something on my shin that looks like red sandpaper, but nothing especially hurts. "Sometimes I have a pain in my thumb?" I say, and Nick yells, "Lytes! Chem 7! Code brown!" I laugh.

"You should use that hand-strengthening ball I gave you," he says.

"I'm just answering your question," I say grouchily. "I don't really want to be assigned any more therapeutic exercises." I sound like my own father.

Nick takes my hand in his own warm hands, rubs gently at the place where my thumb meets my palm. "That feels so good," I say. He tugs on my fingers, massages my wrist, where I can see a few shiny bumps over the bone there. The rash is definitely spreading. "Some of these results don't actually look great," I say, and he says, "I'm sure it will be fine." When I'm quiet, he says, "I'm sorry. I know you hate that—that kind of blanket reassurance." I nod, and he says, "I mean, I do feel like it will be fine? But I always feel like that. I'm sorry you're worried."

"Thank you," I say. "I really appreciate that." We've been together thirty-five years, and we're still getting to know each other. We do not take this project lightly. I mean—sometimes we do? But not always.

"Do you want me to make popcorn?" he says. "And we can turn the air conditioner on and watch *Tiny House Hunters*?" These are a few of my favorite things, and I smile at him.

"I'm okay," I say. "I actually want to look up the rest of these results."

Nick presses his lips together. He would wait for the doctor to interpret them, I know. His personality is very *cross that bridge when you come to it.* Mine is very *apply to engineering school in case there's a bridge that might need crossing but it hasn't been designed yet.*

"Well, then I'll make popcorn for that instead." Nick climbs out of bed. I'm already typing various results into the search engine. Enzymes associated with multiple organ systems. Elevated numbers indicating damaged, leaky cells. Yuck. I picture my cells like a package of chicken at the bottom of the grocery bag, everything around it a little wet from either condensation or actual chicken juice.

Nick is back with popcorn in the vintage gold-colored aluminum bowl we have always used only for popcorn. He's put butter and salt and Frank's Red Hot on it, and it is oily and spicy and a little damp. Perfection. "What are you seeing?"

"I'm not sure," I say. "High levels of these enzymes suggest some kind of injury or disease? But I'm not getting a great read on how high my levels actually are. The low white count is a little terrifying because *leukemia.* But I've had that before. A low white count—not leukemia."

"Yes," Nick says. "I'm aware you've not had leukemia."

"I think I should stop looking," I say, and Nick says, "You know I support that."

"Can I just say one thing?" I say, and Nick says, "Of course."

"If I die, will you please not do the Christmas stockings? Just, like, start a new holiday tradition. I feel like you doing the stockings badly is going to depress the kids even more than not getting them at all."

"Okay," Nick says. "No stockings if you die."

I close my computer, bend over to put it on the floor, and

turn back to Nick. "What do you want to do instead?" I say, and he laughs.

"Put it on," he says. "For me."

"Put *what* on?" I am flirting now, and he knows it. He grabs my wrist, brings my palm to his mouth and kisses it, puts his other hand behind my hip to pull me against him.

Life is so short, isn't it? My ninety-two-year-old father is asleep in the shed, and our daughter is out in the dark, in a car. Our son is in New York City, probably dangling drunk from the tippy-top of the Empire State Building. Miles Zapf is dead; his mother is grieving. Somewhere a train conductor must be studying his own face in the mirror for clues. My body is damaged and leaking and maybe attacking itself for no reason. Or for some reason it hasn't yet divulged. What is there, really, besides disentangling myself from this man so that I can pull from my lingerie drawer the thigh-high striped tube socks and the slinky, strappy nightgown—the one emblazoned with the logo of his favorite hockey team. "Don't look," I say. I'm stuffed with popcorn and dressed like a cross between a goalie and a cheerleader, but when I turn back to the bed, Nick opens his eyes to watch me pull my hair into a high ponytail. "That's my girl," he says, his breath catching, and he opens his arms.

Chapter 12

Willa's home in the middle of the day with a migraine—or maybe just a headache that's threatening to turn into a migraine. She's lying in bed with an ice pack, a glass of cold peppermint tea, and, though she doesn't think she'll need it, the barf bucket: an orange plastic Halloween-candy pail with jack-o'-lantern features. We've used it since the kids were little. "Trick or treat," Nick and I used to say to each other, deadpan, whenever anybody threw up.

You imagine these days are numbered—getting to care for an unwell child—but maybe they're . . . not? I remember worrying that it was the last time I'd get to care for her when she was a high school senior with the flu, a college junior getting her wisdom teeth out, when she got food poisoning the summer after graduation. You touch a cool hand to a hot forehead, rub circles on a clammy back, bring popsicles and Tylenol and a mugful of broth, thinking: *Take care of this precious child while you can.* But here I still am, sitting by the side of the bed—*my* bed—like Marmee March tending her Beth. Also, unrelatedly, I'm on hold with a doctor's office.

"I think this is out of my league now," Dr. Strange had said about the blood results. "I've never seen an ANA that high—I don't even understand how you're walking around."

"Thanks?" I said.

"I don't know about the liver enzymes—those might be inconsequential. But I'm going to refer you to a rheumatologist in Boston. I'll put the referral in today, and they should call you by the end of the week."

You won't be surprised to hear that this is not what has unfolded. Instead, I've been calling both offices, who each claim to be waiting for the other office to do something different. It's a kind of slow-motion standoff, and meanwhile there is a new something on my thighs and upper arms that looks like it's trying to bubble to the surface—the way pancakes get just before it's time to flip them.

The rheumatology scheduler comes back on the line and says, "Yes, no. The referral and requested lab work haven't been faxed to our office yet. We made a note in your portal."

Ah! Yes. At some point I got an email that said I had a note in my portal, only when I clicked on the link I got to a note in my portal that said only, "You have a note in your portal."

Willa points demandingly to Chicken at the bottom of the bed, and I nod, drag him up to her.

"Can I just send them myself?" I ask, and she explains that they must be faxed by the referring office because of confidentiality. This is frustrating because a) Within this very calendar year they will inevitably be sending me an earnestly apologetic letter about how they leaked or sold my personal data, including but not limited to all my biographical information and account numbers as well as, like, my birth certificate and a photo of my vulva that they had on file. And b) Faxing? Really? That's the most secure thing they've got? Back when we still had a fax machine, a random HR office in Idaho sent us a scan of a new hire's social security card—they sent it over and over again, dozens of copies—and I finally had to call, explain that it was a wrong number. Years later, Willa printed a queer zine on the backs of those scans and distributed it to all of her friends. (Sorry, Henry Anderson, 518-55-7978!)

I thank her and hang up.

Willa is whispering to Chicken about what a great and good boy he is and pretend-complaining about his fish breath.

"I have to call the fucking derm office again," I say, and Willa says, "Ugh, Mama."

"Do you need anything before I'm on hold for the rest of my life?"

"Can you bring me Angie too?" she says, and Angie must hear her own name, because here she is suddenly, alighting on the bed on all fours like a furry little Tinker Bell descending from above.

"Was she on the *ceiling?*" Willa says, and I laugh. We don't really understand the physics of Angie. "Oh my god, and she brought Coily!" Coily is the name of her beloved little spring, which came out of a clicky ballpoint pen. Willa tosses Coily, and Angie pounces, scares herself, leaps into the air in a fright, then tips over and falls asleep.

"I missed you so much when you went to college," I say now, apropos of nothing, and Willa says, "Are you talking as you or as a cat?"

"Me," I say.

"I missed you too," she says. I lift her hand, kiss the back of it.

"I'll probably leave again, though, Mama," she says, and I make myself smile.

"I know you will," I say.

I dial the dermatologist's number, navigate the main menu like a pro, but get put immediately on hold. Willa sips her tea and reads on her phone about migraine headaches—curious about what they even are, from a neurological perspective. I stop myself from asking her to google how often a migraine turns out to be an occult or bursting brain aneurysm because this is a bad neighborhood in my mind that nobody else should be led into. I must surely have suffered from anxiety before the kids were born, but I don't even remember it that well. Back then it was just cranky concerns about lost luggage or that the guy taking my order at the bagel place hadn't heard me ask for capers on my toasted everything with a schmear, rather than this obliterative fear of death.

Willa interrupts her research to complain. "I inherited every bad thing from you," she says, and I grimace because it's true. Allergies, migraines, hammertoes, cystic acne, anxiety.

"I'm sorry, honey," I say. "If it's any consolation, I inherited it all from Grandma."

"It's not any consolation," she says.

She reads to me a little from the basic theories about vasoconstriction and vasodilation. She tells me about prodrome— the *before* feeling—and I keep to myself the tidbit shared by a doctor friend of mine: that a feeling of euphoria often precedes the migraine itself. Now every time I'm happy I wonder if I'm about to get the worst headache of my life, which is pretty much a perfect metaphor for the way I experience happiness as the likelihood of another shoe dropping into a pile of shit. Willa, still reading, comes to a description of the four phases of a migraine. "Oh my god, she says, "I mean, okay, yeah, *aura*—bright lights, blind spots, yadda yadda, fine. But get this: 'Others may experience the sensation of being grabbed or fondled.' Are you fucking kidding me?"

"I didn't grope you," I say. "That was your *migraine aura*."

"Oh, you woke up with my cock in your mouth?" Willa says. "Sounds like a *migraine sensation*. Jesus fucking Christ. How are any of us even still alive?"

We are still laughing the laughter of the funny and doomed when I hold up a finger because the dermatology referrals coordinator is back. I describe the problem, and he explains that they've done everything correctly on their end—it's all very *Groundhog Day* so far—and then I ask if we can just double-check that they have the right fax number for the rheumatologist. He reads me the number, and the last two digits are switched. "Oh!" I say cheerfully, in lieu of screaming. "That's actually the wrong number. Those last two digits are four-seven, not seven-four."

I read the correct number aloud in its entirety and he says, "Yes, that's the number we've been trying."

"Ah, I think it might not be," I say. "You actually just read me a different number."

"I didn't," he says. "That's the same number. I don't know why it's not going through. We can try it one more time if you want. But I can't keep doing this." While he's scolding me, somebody somewhere is probably drafting their last will and testament on the back of my antinuclear antibody test results.

"Please do," I say. "But can you please just make sure that you reenter the number correctly?" There's the click of disconnection, and I lie back on the bed and try not to cry.

"Oh my god," I say. "I really just can't even. And of course it's a fucking *man*."

Willa opens her eyes, narrows them at me.

"Sorry, sorry," I say. I'm trying not to be such a gender essentialist. "I just mean someone with a penis," I clarify. No, no, no. "An anatomically *attached* penis," I add, apologetically. "The kind that would bleed if you cut it." What is wrong with me? "I mean, you *wouldn't* cut it? But it, you know, has its own blood supply."

"Mom, oh my god. Please stop," Willa says. She's laughing. "I was just spacing out. But are you trying to say *cis man*? You don't actually know that's what he is. But feel free to cut his penis and check."

"I fucking *might*," I say, and she laughs.

"I think my headache's better," she says. "I should probably go back to work." She sits up, stands up, walks out the door—and now there's just an empty glass, an empty bucket, and a thawing ice pack where before there was a girl. A woman, I suppose.

I call the rheumatology scheduler. They haven't received any faxes.

Chapter 13

I'm sautéing finely diced vegetables in the big Dutch oven when the kitchen door opens and my dad ambles in.

"Good morning, daughter," he says. "I was lured by the fragrance of onions." He sits with a groan.

"I'm making short ribs," I say, and he says, "Ahhhh, my very favorite."

"They should be ready in a mere four hours," I say.

My dad laughs, says, "Then I should probably have a snack."

"What can I get you?" I say, and he says, "No, no. I'll get it myself. I'm going to get up and make a little lunch. In five minutes." Forty-five years ago, he would have said, *As soon as I finish this cigarette.*

"Do you want one of your hot dogs?" I say, and he considers, then says, "I don't think so. They should be fine if you give them a good hard boil, but they're definitely getting a little ripe."

"But help yourself," he adds.

I offer him coffee, but he says he made some earlier in the shack. "Not a prizewinning cup," he admits. "Certainly not as good as Mom's." I think it was Freud who defined *nostalgia* as a longing for something you never had in the first place. My mom's coffee was simultaneously weak and punishing. Like if you melted a brown crayon into a mug of boiling water and then added half-and-half, only one of the halves was sulfuric acid. *I miss your mother* is all he's trying to say. "I miss her too," I say, and he smiles.

Outside our kitchen window, the maples are smudging from green to yellow to orange to red, each tree perfectly variegated. It's the first day cool enough to leave the oven on for so long.

I squeeze a little tomato paste into the mirepoix and let it cook until it browns, then scrape everything onto a plate. I put the pot back over the flame with a slick of bacon fat, let it heat up while I dredge the meat in flour and salt.

"Did you see that story made the national news now?" my dad says, and I say, "What story?" but I don't know why I say that. I know what story.

"That kid and the train," he says. "The *Times* ran something about it."

"Why?" I say. The last thing I saw online was a letter to the editor of our local paper suggesting that the conductor was stoned at the time of the accident, although this was speculation—and it was probably a veiled complaint about how every storefront in our town is now The Hempest or RESIN8 or Terp 'n Tine or Cheech & Chong's Dispensoria. I lay each piece of meat in the hot fat, and it sizzles and spatters.

I HAVE TOLD NOBODY THAT I went to the funeral. Well, not the funeral itself, but the cemetery, afterward. Miles's mother had put up an announcement on Facebook, so I knew it wasn't private, but I understood that I was being a creep nonetheless.

There were lots of people I recognized: teachers, a few parents, our pediatrician, a handful of kids whose names I didn't know. I loitered out of view like one of those people in a movie who comes to a funeral they don't belong at because they're a mafia hitman or a ghost. I had reasons for being there, sure, but none of them were good. *Proximity to the thing I'm most afraid of. A strong sense that I know how it might feel to lose a child. Marinating in someone else's grief like it could season me to the bone.* But if you don't express it, then who does empathy even serve? I couldn't hear what they were saying, but I could feel it wafting off of her, his mother. Like a vapor. The way she was entirely made from sorrow now, dragging her body around not because she was attached to the idea of life but simply because she couldn't shake it.

"IT WAS PART OF A bigger story about cost-cutting measures the railroad companies are taking," my dad is telling me. "They're laying people off, postponing repairs. That kind of thing. They used the Zapf story to show the kind of problems they've created—more accidents, shoddier oversight, a general distrust of the whole enterprise."

Willa and her friend Sunny burst into the kitchen, and I shush my dad. I am hoping Willa has more or less forgotten about this story. I don't want her to be fretful and obsessed.

"I thought you guys were still sleeping," I say, and Willa says, "No, we were collecting pretty leaves. Do we still have wax paper? Where's the iron? We want to make those window decorations."

"The kindergarten kind," Sunny says, her eyes gold and

green and sparkling. They're both wearing jeans, flip-flops, and old rugby shirts of Nick's. Sunny's hair is pulled up into a messy bun, the bleached ends fraying out of it.

"Wax paper in the foil drawer," I say. "Iron in the basement, on the floor, by the ironing board." I'm turning all the meat over with tongs, admiring the deep brown crust on it.

"That's a whole lot of meat smell," Willa says, and I say, "I'm going to make you that tofu you like, the mock au vin kind with the herbs and the wine. Mashed potatoes too."

"Yum," she says. "Aha!" She has found the wax paper.

"Rocky, can I help with anything?" Sunny asks, and I say, "Yes, would you brown this meat and then make my dad some lunch?" She laughs. She lived here for most of a year during high school and is not exactly a guest.

"She's kidding, Sonya," my dad says to her. He uses her full given name even though nobody else seems to. "I'm going to scramble myself an egg. In five minutes."

"You want a scrambled egg?" Willa says. "I got you, Grandpa."

"Really?" my dad says. "That would be lovely."

I pour half a bottle of pinot noir into the pot, and it sputters and boils while I scrape at the bottom with a wooden spoon. Willa stands beside me to heat the egg pan, and Sunny sits next to my dad on the couch to sort the leaves by color.

My dad emits a sudden grunt of disapproval.

"What?" I say.

"Jamie," he says. "I texted him to see if he wanted that beautiful dinner table of ours and he said he didn't." Jamie and Maya live in a New York City one-bedroom apartment the size of our one-car garage. The only place you would maybe be able to put a dining table is the kitchen, but you can't, because there's a bathtub there. My parents' dining table is an enormous carved-walnut affair with twelve chairs. It would not look out of place in a castle or a haunted boarding school.

"I can't believe he doesn't like it," my dad is saying. "That table has universal appeal."

Willa, scrambling my dad's egg next to me, laughs. "Mom," she says quietly. "Don't get into it with him."

"Dad," I say. "Dad." I am! I am getting into it with him! "First of all—did he actually say he didn't like it? I find that hard to imagine." Jamie is a puppy of a person—all friendliness and agreeable curiosity. "And second of all—nothing has *universal appeal*. That's not a thing. People have different taste, around the world, across history, for a million different reasons. Their apartment is furnished mostly from IKEA. It's kind of hard to picture your table there."

"I wasn't meaning to set you off, Rachel," my dad says coolly. "It sounds like you're not a big fan of the table either."

"No, ugh." I'm scraping the vegetables back into the pot now, pushing my hair off my face with the back my hand. "Dad, I have a ton of affection for that table. I just feel defensive for Jamie."

"Well, he was a little harsh is all," he says grumpily and shrugs.

Willa is buttering my dad's toast, and she laughs. "Grandpa, what did Jamie write? What *exactly*?"

I add a sprig of thyme and a bay leaf to the pot, put the lid on, and pop it in the oven. Come dinnertime, the meat will fall all to pieces if you so much as look at it, and it will taste of wine and salt and long heat. The potatoes will be smooth and buttery, the tofu braised and savory and kind to animals. I'll toss together a crisp green salad, dress it sharply, and we will sit at the table together and know the meaning of life.

A sheepish look passes over my dad's face before he reads Jamie's text out loud. "What a lovely offer, Grandpa," our son has written. "Maya and I really wish we had room for that table. We have such fond memories of eating all of Grandma's wonderful meals there. Thank you so much for thinking of us. Look forward to seeing you later this month."

Willa laughs, says, "Wow! That *is* harsh!" She hands my dad a plate of eggs and toast, a fork, a napkin. He thanks her. "I hear that it doesn't sound so bad," he admits, and I say, because I know how it feels to hurt your own feelings, "Sometimes things just feel bad anyways."

Chapter 14

" Like there's a miniature soccer game and a miniature coach is blowing his miniature whistle over and over again. No, no. Like a hamster wheel, but soothing."

We're sitting in camp chairs by the firepit, and my friend Jo has been trying, for the last half hour or so, to describe the way the crickets sound to her. It's just the two of us—Nick is home with Willa and my dad, and Jo's doctor husband, Davey, is on call—and we are very, very stoned. I have been laughing so hard that I have to keep wiping my eyes with the sleeve of my sweatshirt.

JO AND I HAVE BEEN friends since our older children were in the same preschool class. All four of our kids went to the same elementary, middle, and high school, the same pediatrician, the same single week of half-day farm camp. The kids grew up together; Jo and I grew up together as mothers. We went on the same field trips to the local fire station, to the Boston art museum, to this or that living history reenactment site ("There were colonial *rabbis*?" Jo's kid Amelia whispered to me once, pointing, and I had to tell her that they were just regular present-day Hassidim here from the city.) We threw joint birthday parties and filled goody bags with the particular category of plastic items Jo called *trish-trash*. We worried together—about stupid stuff (in the event, the baby's teeth *would* grow in) and terrifying stuff (depression, anxiety, self-harm) and our occasionally flailing marriages. We started running; we stopped running. We started Zumba, which we still do. We text recipes and stain-removal tips like housewives from a different era. We decided to drink less. We emptied our nests at the same time, and then watched them fill back up: I have Willa and my dad and the cats now; Jo's got Amelia, two dogs, and a rabbit someone left on her front step in a box with a note that said, PLEASE, JO.

"DON'T TAKE THIS THE WRONG way, but do you have a, like, unusually large forehead?" Jo says suddenly, and I put a hand to it.
 "Not to my knowledge," I say, and she laughs, says, "No offense. It just looks kind of weird all of a sudden."
 "Yours a little bit does too," I admit, and she laughs more.
 "ET phone home," she says, and I say, "Oh my god. Exactly."
 "Are we all just walking around with these massive foreheads?" she says. "That's so tragic!"
 On and off all night, the logs in the fire have looked to me like there's writing on them, letters scrolling across the glowing embers in a kind of neon cursive. I keep forgetting that this is just me being stoned, and have mentioned the mysterious messages more than once. "That log totally sucks," I say now, by accident. "'Life is not a dress reversal,'" I read aloud. "What the fuck?"
 Jo laughs so hard her chair falls over sideways against the

cooler. "I'm peeing my pants again," she says. She's actually wheezing now. "Come to the bathroom with me. I feel like I'm just going to keep getting lost out there." She has already wandered, laughing and apologizing, through multiple other campsites. The last time she went to pee she came back with a tofu hot dog in a bun.

"Aha!" I say. "I will. I have just the thing!" I flip the switch on the Instagram lantern, and it's as perfectly picturesque as I imagined. "Come," I say to Jo, beckoning. I'm wearing a long flannel nightgown, holding the light by its curved wooden handle.

Jo stands up to bend over and laugh a little more. "Oh my god," she says. "You look like—" I laugh too, because I know what she's going to say because I can literally read her mind right now!

"I know what you're going to say!" I say telepathically but out loud. "I can literally read your mind right now!"

"What?" she says.

"That I look like Ebenezer Scrooge." I bend over in my nightie, with the lantern, and cry, "Bah humbug!"

"That's not what I was going to say," she says.

"I am as merry as a schoolboy!" I say. "God bless us, every one!"

"Oh my god, Rocky, stop," she says. She's crying again. "I was going to say—" She's on her hands and knees on the pine-needle path to the bathroom, laughing so hard she can't speak for a full minute. "I was going to say you look like Wee Willie Winkie."

In the dimly lit, moth-encrusted bathroom, in our separate stalls, we try to pull ourselves together, although I keep whispering, "Tapping at the window, crying at the lock," and other Wee Willie Winkie–isms to make Jo laugh. A mom comes in with a clutch of tooth-brushing children, and we go silent. We don't want to spook anybody. "Apparently I finished peeing before we even got in here," Jo announces from her stall, and then she says, "Shit, sorry, I didn't realize I was saying that out loud," and then, "Oh, shit, excuse my language. I'm so sorry." When we come out of our stalls, three little girls look up at us with big eyes and the mom laughs.

IT'S CRAZY THAT I'M INTO pot again. The last time I smoked it was 1990 and Nick was handing me a ten-foot-long plastic bong covered in Grateful Dead stickers and I inhaled until my lungs fell out. We accidentally bought oregano glued to a popsicle stick and, in lieu of smoking it, we scraped it into our spaghetti; we accidentally bought oat straw ground up with cocaine and woke up in a neighbor's barn. It wasn't for me, I thought. I thought this for decades.

I started up again last winter because I was trying to drink less, and there was a learning curve. The first time I smoked just the littlest bit, and Nick and I played Yahtzee and went for a walk in the falling snow and had the kind of sex that is less like a moaning operatic duet and more like a merry bout of Hide the Salami. The second time I ate part of an infused chocolate at a reggae show before I decided it wasn't working and ate the rest and came to on the slushy sidewalk with Nick and Jo squatting down beside me, laughing fondly and singing along to "I Shot the Sheriff." Nick sent a photo to our family group chat. *Rookie mistake, Mama*, Jamie texted back, along with a string of cry-laughing emojis and, for the next several months, many memes about edibles kicking in.

Now I walk right into the dispensary and star in a one-act play called *Your Mom Is Getting High!* The kids working there are as knowledgeable and courteous as sommeliers discussing the finer points of this or that *flower*, as they call it. "I want to feel like I drank about one and a half beers," I explained on my first expedition. "Whatever the THC equivalent is. Big, strong beers," I clarified. "I got you," the dispenser said—and he did. I came away with a chalky low-dose lemon-lime candy, which my kids call granny vitamins.

When I was at Danks a Lot to stock up before camping, I couldn't help myself. "Do you ever drive high?" I asked, and the *budtender* raised his eyebrows and shook his head. "Ugh, sorry," I said. "I'm not, like, being your mom. I'm just curious about the mechanics of it. Like, if you drove high, do you think you'd be much more likely to get in an accident?"

"I would never do it," he said.

"Of course," I said. "Of course not. I am just thinking—okay. Not a car. But, like, what if you were doing something a little less hands-on? Like driving—I don't know. A train?" Now I was starring in a one-act play called *Your Mom Is an Amateur Detective!*

"*Stoned*, you know?" the budtender said opaquely.

"Yes," I said. I'd been in there for five minutes, and already I could smell the skunky weed smell in my hair. "I mean, no. What do you mean?"

"I mean—like—that's the point of the ganja, right? Slowwww it down, my sister. So, yeah, probably something where you're just chilling, you've got your conductor hat on, the window's open. A little breeze. It's nice. Maybe you blow your train whistle, you've got some Doritos—"

"Thank you," I said. Now he was just picturing *Dazed and Confused*, but railroad themed. Had I imagined he was going to produce a scientific monograph on impaired response times? "If you had to do something quickly, though—like, put on the brakes—could you?"

He tipped his head on the skinny stalk of his neck and looked directly into my eyes. "Are you talking about that accident?" he said. "Miles Zapf?"

"Not really," I lied. "I mean—kind of?"

"I knew him," he said, and I thought: *Of course.*

"I'm so sorry," I said.

"No, it's all good," he said, the way young people do about the worst possible things. *It's all good,* they say, when you've got a bloody fork in your hand and their eyeball's been accidentally poked out onto the floor. "But I know what you mean. I read it too—the letter in the paper," he said. "The owner sent it around because it was kind of about cannabis, like, as a *business*?"

"Oh," I say. "What did you think?"

He shrugged. "I don't know," he said. "That train should've stopped anyway. Even if the conductor was drunk or stoned or sleeping, it should've. Why do you care?" He asked this not in the hostile *What's it to you?* way, but as an actual question. Why did I care?

"I guess I can't stand the idea that one person would have to feel responsible for something so awful," I said truthfully. Someone lying in bed at night, smothered under a blanket of guilt? Imagining the sorrow they've caused? Wishing they could return to a single moment and avert disaster? There's nothing worse. Almost nothing.

He nodded, smiled. "You're Jamie's mom," he said.

I smiled back. "I am."

"Jamie's my dude," he said.

"In a weed-buying way?" I said, and he laughed.

"High school jazz," he said. "From back in the day. Bass." He air-guitared a little bass, and I almost remembered him. "Jamie's a good dude," he added, and I felt smugly pleased, thanked him, and left with my vitamins.

BACK IN OUR TENT, JO and I discover that we are not the rowdiest people at the campground.

"You are *shitting* on Cran-Apple right now, and I don't know why," a drunk guy is saying sadly, loudly, at the site next to ours. "It's my favorite juice drink and you are literally shitting on it."

"*Literally?*" Jo whispers. "I mean—ew?"

"You are literally shitting on my Cran-Apple right now," the man says again, and Jo gruntingly pantomimes holding a bottle up to her own asshole.

"I'm not shitting on it," a woman says, all the words slurred together. "I'm calling it *Crap*-Apple because it fucking suuuuuucks."

"But its's my favorite juice drink," the guy says sorrowfully.

"It's hard to be a person," I whisper, and Jo says, "Bah humbug," and chuckles herself to sleep.

Chapter 15

"These are most likely different morphologies of a single process," the rheumatologist is saying. "Whatever is causing any of the rash is probably causing all of it."

She gestures at my legs, my arms, both of which are poking out of the blue fabric johnny, and both of which are now covered—ankle to hip, wrist to armpit—with different morphologies of a single process. In some places it's flat and dark, like a child has pressed a pencil eraser onto a purple inkpad and stamped out masses of overlapping bruise-colored circles; in other places it's crusty and pink or weeping and red or even, on my shoulders, yellow and blistering, like the gaseous, steaming, egg-smell puddles Nick and I nearly fell into at Yellowstone Park. Nothing hurts, though. Nothing even itches.

"I'm going to biopsy this one site, on your upper arm. Just to see if we can extract a little more information," she says.

While she preps, punches, stitches, she explains some of what I already know about granulomas—the way they're clumped clusters of cells. "The thing is," she says, "once your body starts making granulomas? It gets very excited about making granulomas. It just wants to make more and more of them—it's all a little haywire." I picture a factory cranking out endless little fleshy blobs—cellular peanut clusters—with Lucy and Ethel cramming them into their mouths in a panic.

"So other people's bodies are making, like, biceps and triceps and babies, and mine's making, just, white beard hairs and these?" She laughs.

"Are you using the hydrocortisone cream your dermatologist prescribed?" She's looking at something on her computer.

"I am," I say. The more rash I have, though, the longer it takes to spread the cream onto it. It reminds me of the urban myth about the Golden Gate Bridge: by the time they finish painting it, it's time to start over. "In fact, it's kind of all I do now," I say. "Put cream on my rash." *Oh, I'd love to,* I'll start saying when people invite me anywhere. *But I have to put cream on my rash that night.*

"Is it helping?" she says, then looks up and shakes her head. "Sorry. I'm going to guess *no*. You can stop using it."

This should be a relief to me, but, instead, it's alarming. "Are we just giving up?" I say. If she feeds me a broiled chicken leg and then removes my collar, buries her face in my fur, and cries, I'll know the vet is coming to put me down.

"No, no," she says. She is much younger than me and her skin is clear and dewy. When she smiles, I can see her pretty teeth: white and straight with a little gap in front. "I'm going to prescribe you something different. An oral medication that should help with the underlying inflammation—although it can take a long time to start working. A couple months. Hydroxychloroquine. It's a very old, well-studied drug. You should tolerate it without incident."

She stands up from her wheelie stool, takes one of my hands

in hers and looks at it—rubs her thumb across the knuckles. She looks directly into my eyes.

"How do you feel?" she asks, and I'm so taken aback by the question that I bow my head and cry a little. "Good," I say.

She passes me a tissue from the box within reach. "That's good," she says, and I say, like a very small, crying child, "This thumb hurts."

"Okay," she says. She gently releases the hand she's holding and picks up the hurting one, bends the thumb back and forth, looks at the knuckle, places the hand back in my lap.

I wipe my whole face with the tissue. "What's your best guess?" I say. "About what this is?"

She nods thoughtfully, sits, and wheels back over to her desk. "I'd be very surprised if it wasn't something autoimmune. Lupus is the strongest possibility—maybe cutaneous lupus, which means just your skin is involved." She's looking at her computer again. "Some of the results here are very suggestive of lupus—especially the ANA, some of these other antibodies too. Some don't *quite* fit. One is more suggestive of a clotting issue. I'm going to schedule you for a biopsy of one of your lymph nodes."

"Wait," I say. My blood cools in my veins. Probably it is already clotting, congealing. "What?"

She's mousing over something on her screen. "They sent you for a follow-up after your last mammogram, it looks like."

"Yes," I say, remembering. In the waiting room they'd hung an enlarged color photo of a pansy upside down, which was disconcerting with respect to their accuracy. "That's right. But it turned out to be nothing."

She nods in a not-quite-nodding way. "It turned out not to

be suggestive of breast cancer," she says. "But it is something. An enlarged lymph node in your armpit. There are a couple of them, it looks like. The radiologist did not flag it as an area of especial concern—and it's overwhelmingly likely to be inconsequential," she says. "But given some of the anomalies in your blood work, I just want to be absolutely certain."

"Absolutely certain of what?" I say.

"Absolutely certain that we're not looking at a lymphoproliferative disorder," she says. "Though I don't think that we are."

"Lymphoma," I say. "Leukemia." I am nothing if not a scholar of my own demise.

She shrugs. "Or something like multiple myeloma," she says. "Though, again, I would be very, very surprised. We're just ruling it out from the get-go so we can move forward with absolute confidence. My best guess is that the hydroxychloroquine is going to start treating the rash before we even get to the lymph node—and that's going to be another clue that it's an immunologic process."

"I have such a bad feeling," I say. "Am I going to end up dead?"

Is Willa just going to have to—what? Freeze her own ice packs when she gets a headache? I picture Nick and the kids standing in a bereaved, besuited clump, receiving consoling words, meaningful eye contact, kisses on the cheek, norovirus. And my dad. No. My mind goes protectively blank. I do need to outlive my father.

"Eventually," she says and smiles. "But no time soon, I hope."

BACK OUT IN THE WAITING room I cry briefly when Nick stands to greet me, refuse to answer any of his questions, and ask him to invite me to lunch.

"Let me take you to lunch," he says, and I say, "I'm not really hungry."

"Come on," he says. "I'll take you to Sofra." Sofra is the café where they put five different dips on a plate for you—beet-pink tzatziki, silky hummus, eggplant mashed with herbs and lemon, spiced labneh, and pomegranate-sweetened roasted peppers blitzed with walnuts—and then they give you a big, warm, soft pita for scooping it all up with. It is my actual favorite.

"Hm," I say, considering. "Okay."

He holds my hand on the way to the parking garage.

"I probably have lymphoma," I say. "Also subcutaneous lupus and different morphologies and multiple myeloma. A congealing disorder."

Nick lets go of my hand to put his arm around my horrible, suppurating shoulders.

"Ugh," he says, laughing softly. "So many things!"

I stop walking to turn into his arms, burst into tears. We stand on the sidewalk and he rocks me a little while I cry onto his warm chest and complain that he's rubbing my biopsy wound. "Okay," he says. "Shhhh. It's okay, my love. Shoot—sorry. Did that hurt? Shhhh. I've got you. Whatever this is—we'll get through it." The comforting platitudes of the ignorant and the damned, which comfort me nonetheless.

"What are you going to put in the kids' Christmas stockings?" I say, my face still pressed into his good-smelling T-shirt, and he says, "Nothing." He squeezes me. "Nice try, though."

Chapter 16

Nick wakes halfway up to see what I'm looking at on my phone in the dark. It's a sculpture that Miles Zapf's mother has posted to Facebook—a clay figure with an expression of grief so pure it's nearly ecstatic: head tipped back, mouth stretched open, arms cradling a kind of infinite emptiness. The caption reads: *Lost Mother.* I'm scrolling through the comments to see if she made it herself. It looks like she did.

"Maybe don't quit your day job for full-time sculpting, amirite?" Nick says, and then, a second later, "Oh, shit! Are you crying? I'm sorry, honey. I don't even have my glasses on. What are you looking at?" He wraps an arm around my waist, dislodging Chicken, who stretches and sighs, and they both resume snoring.

An email dings in, and it's an Amazon order. The kids still use my account because of the free shipping, and I always look to see what they're getting. This is going to Jamie in New York, and it's a fire extinguisher. I screenshot it, text it to Jamie, write, *I'm guessing there's a story here.*

You don't want to know, he writes back with a cry-laughing emoji.

Can't sleep? I write.

Because of the fire, he writes.

I laugh out loud, write, *lol*.

You want this? I write, and text him a screenshot from the Buy Nothing group where someone has offered up "a single (large) slice of Hubbard squash for gifting."

That really *would* make a great gift! Jamie writes.

I'll grab it for you, I write, and Jamie writes, *Thank you! The only thing better than a whole Hubbard squash is *part of* a Hubbard squash.*

You want? he texts, with a screenshot from the NYC Buy Nothing group, where a used bottle of molasses is on offer. *It's very VERY sweet*, the gifter has warned, and someone has written, irritably, *Yes, because it's molasses.*

Or this? Jamie writes. This photo appears to be one of actual garbage: crumpled paper and foil; plastic wrappers and packing peanuts; something that looks like coffee grounds. *Recycle it into your art and keep it out of the landfill!* is the accompanying admonishment, and ten people have written, *Interested*.

I miss you so much it feels like all my ribs are bruised, I write and delete. And then, since nobody's here to accuse me of being a needy, emotional pest, I write, *Hey, honey, did you hear about Miles Zapf?*

Three dots appear, then nothing, then three dots.

Sorry, sorry, I write. *I'm sure you did. No need to respond.*

No, no, he writes. The three dots again. Then, *Yeah, I did.*

It's so sad, I write, like a dumbass, and he writes, *Yeah*.

Chapter 17

I'm washing the inexplicable sinkful of dishes that accumulates between lunch and dinner. It's mostly mugs and glasses and small plates covered in crumbs and knives slicked with peanut butter. My dad is on the kitchen couch with Willa, trying to remember the name of a friend he played bridge with back in New York. Willa is no help at all.

"Stu?" he says. "Not Stu. Skew? That's not even a name."

"Do you want to just tell us whatever you wanted to tell us?" Willa asks. "Just call him Skew for the sake of the story."

"I am trying to look it up on my phone," my dad says, and Willa leans over to look and says, "Grandpa, all you've typed is the word *stew*. It's just pictures of meat and vegetables."

I turn to dry my hands on a dish towel and see their heads bent together, hers as glossy and dark-capped as a chickadee and his an evaporating fluff of white. My heart fills up, spills over, fills again. A river rushing its banks. It's something like love, but more dangerous.

"You know who I mean," he says to me, and I say, "I never really met your bridge friends, Dad."

"That's true," he says. "It'll come to me. Stu? Sue? That's not a man's name. He became a Diamond Life Master just before I did. He wasn't well. He had those"—he pauses to think—"pimply innards."

Willa laughs. "Pimply innards?"

"You know what I mean," my dad says opaquely. "Give me a second. His name—it's going to bubble up to the surface if I stop trying so hard."

I know this exact feeling. I can be on my mental hands and knees, flailing around under the couch of my mind with a hockey stick, trying to sweep out a name I can't remember—and all I'll dredge up is a Ping-Pong ball, a catnip mouse, and a spool of thread. If I look away, though, sometimes it might creep out on its own little feet.

"Hieronymus!" my dad announces suddenly, and Willa says, "Actually?"

"Yes," my dad says.

"In the event, a name not overly similar to *stew*," Willa says, and my dad shakes his head, shrugs.

"He went by Jerry."

"And?" Willa says.

My dad sighs. "I don't remember what I wanted to tell you about him."

I'm lacing up my sneakers by the door. "Come on a walk with me," I say. "Both of you. I want to get outside before I start dinner. I've been working on those stupid spatchcocking edits all day."

"Maybe I'll come just as far as the cul-de-sac," my dad says.

"Great," I say.

"Give me five minutes," my dad says, and I sigh.

"Can it be more like *one* minute?" I say. The light is fading already.

Willa catches my eye and smiles a smile that means, *Your father is ninety-two years old, so could you please muster a single fucking modicum of patience?* and I smile back a smile that means, *No.*

"Go without me," he says, not unkindly, and I say, "No, no, Dad. Five minutes is good."

OUT ON THE STREET, FIFTEEN minutes later, the brown smell of the leaves is everywhere, as are the many towering headless plastic skeletons, every skull tucked into the crook of a fleshless elbow.

My dad frees his arm from Willa's to gesture at one. "I don't find those very attractive," he says, and we say us either. Puddles on the pavement reflect the bright autumn colors.

A new neighbor's gorgeous baby is out on the sidewalk in a pram, alone, and we coo and babble. When the neighbor emerges from her house, I cry, "Finders keepers!" and pantomime running away with the baby carriage. She lunges toward me, laughing nervously, and pushes the carriage back inside.

"Sorry, sorry," I yell after her. "Totally kidding, of course!"

"Oh my god, Mom," Willa says. "She doesn't know us well enough for you to make a *kidnapping* joke."

"I have bad judgment," I say sadly.

"Me too," my dad says and pats me.

He turns back for home at the circle. Willa and I bend right onto the path and are swallowed up immediately by the woods. We walk in comfortable silence for a while, pointing out this or that thing to each other: a white mushroom with its frilled cap flipped up like Marilyn Monroe's famous dress; goldenrod, crisping now in the early chill; the poison ivy revealing itself in all its autumn garishness: shocking red garlands snaking around the maple trunks. "Were there always all these heavy vines choking the trees?" Willa asks, and I say I don't think so. The jewelweed is covered in plump seedpods, like miniature sugar snap peas; you can hold one in your closed fist and feel it explode gently into a chaos of green coils and tiny walnut-flavored seeds, which we pick out of each other's palms and eat. We share a handful of speckly red autumn olives—berries that are bitterly tart and only faintly fruity. Willa and I love them. "I feel like you must get your entire daily allowance of some nutrient from this," I say, and Willa says, her face puckered, "Is that nutrient *acid*?"

I make her imitate the birds.

"What did that one say?" I say, and Willa says, "Yikyakyik-yak."

"That one?" And she says, "Chee chee chee CHAAAA."

Sometimes we're just walking, not talking at all, the leaves ruckling and crunching under our shoes.

IF YOU HAD TOLD ME, when Willa was fifteen, that it would ever be like this, I would have thought you were pranking me just to be mean. Back then, every molecule in her body recoiled, in horror, from every molecule in my own. I exhaled carbon dioxide that she was then *forced to inhale*! I manifested odors and opinions and existence, and all of it was unspeakable, intolerable. I felt, for a year or two, like I was kneeling soundlessly with a palmful of birdseed, hand extended, waiting for the wild animal of my daughter to approach me.

"You are the keeper of her secrets," Nick said to me once, in the interest of consolation. "Her closest, most trusted person. She has to hate you sometimes." He, meanwhile, was permitted to take her roller-skating and out for gelato. She lolled in his lap, eyeing me coolly, and I could only beam my enormous love out to her in silent waves. I was a lighthouse for one ship, but that ship was sightless and, I feared, already tossed up on the rocks.

NOW I'M TRYING TO SHOW her a stinkhorn mushroom and she says, "Oh my god! Stop trying to make me look at all the penis-y things."

"Touch it," I say, and she shakes her head but extends one finger to touch it anyway and screams when it ejaculates a cloud of spore. "You suck," she says, laughing. I really do!

We are rounding the back of the neighboring farm, turning for home, the sun setting in gold bars between the black trunks of the trees. *Just this, now*, I think. I seriously do not give a single flying fuck what that no-Zen editor thinks! That really is all there is—this moment, here, with my beautiful daughter in the beautiful world. Even if, yes, I'm a little spooked. *The biopsy shows an unusual constellation of findings*, the Boston dermatopathologist has written in my portal, *and I am not certain of the diagnosis*. There are *sarcoidal-type granulomas, multiple foci of necrotizing granulomatous dermatitis, a prominent associated lymphocytic component*, and *vasculopathy with thrombosis*. The results are not typical of lupus, he has noted, nor of any other granulomatous disease familiar to him. He concludes that *the findings raise the possibility of another unclassified disease process*.

A universe full of stars, and I have a constellation of findings that is no constellation at all. You can connect them, sure, but only to form a picture of nothingness and uncertainty. *See those six stars? Right there*, a mother might say to a child, pointing up into the punctured black bowl of the night. *That's Lupus! And those over there—that's one of the Familiar Granulomatous Diseases! What about the rest?* the child might say, gesturing to the random, spreading smear of endless spots. But it's an unclassified disease process, and it has no name.

The results have prompted the rheumatologist to add a new drug into the mix—methotrexate—and to refer me to a specialized granulomatous disease clinic, with whose scheduling department I have already been on hold for the better part of a decade. My lymph-node biopsy is on the books for next week.

"Mama, can I say something weird and kind of stressful that's a non sequitur?" Willa says.

"Of course," I say. She's such a mind reader that I'm worried she's going to ask about the biopsy results in my portal. I'd put her and Sunny in charge of the suture removal, which they accomplished with sewing scissors and tweezers and a minor excess of conspiratorial joy. They sterilized everything with vanilla-flavored vodka. I winced when it stung, and Sunny, who's applying to medical school, worried aloud that they were hurting me. Willa swished her hand and said, "Please. She's fine. She's just being a drama queen for no reason."

"I'm still thinking about Miles Zapf," Willa says now, and I say, "Me too, honey."

"I keep looking at his Facebook account and stuff. I've read all the news. I looked at his LinkedIn profile. Jamie's high school yearbook." She's still walking, not looking at me. She runs her hands over her short hair, then pulls them up into the sleeves of her hoodie. "It's not like you could know, but I feel so sure he didn't mean to kill himself. His mother said he didn't leave a note or anything—that he was driving back from contra dancing. He'd texted her about it. That he was on his way home. I feel like the train people are leaning into the suicide angle so it won't be their fault."

"I feel like that too," I say.

She shakes her head. "I don't know," she says. "I guess I just want to stop thinking about the accident. The teeth of my brain have really sunk into it, though."

"I hear you, chick. Do you want to set up an appointment with Dr. Shrinky-Dink?" This is Willa's therapist.

"Yeah, probably," she says. She shakes her head. "I don't know. I'll figure it out."

Willa stops walking and points to the deep, burning orange that is settling low between the trees. "Look!" she says. "It's so pretty."

"So pretty," I echo.

"I wonder why it's adaptive for humans to like sunsets," she says. "Like, thinking a setting sun is pretty—why is that a heritable trait? How does it help with genetic continuation?"

"I don't know," I say.

"Maybe it reminds you that you should be building a fire," she hypothesizes. "If you think a sunset's pretty, then you want to see more of it, so you build a fire that kind of looks like it."

"And then you don't freeze to death or get salmonella from

eating raw voles. Or maybe," I say, "we just think it's pretty because it's pretty." She snorts.

"It's not *mystical*," she says. "It's science—whether or not we know the science."

"Maybe it's both," I say, and she starts walking again, says, "It's definitely not."

Chapter 18

I'm back in Boston for the lymph-node biopsy, lying on the gurney in a blue johnny and a pair of disposable yellow no-skid socks. My rash is everywhere, and I am trying not to feel self-conscious—surely they've seen worse here in the hospital!—but I notice people steal glances at it as they pass by, wondering if I'm a rotting corpse that's been exhumed from a crypt after first being murdered with an industrial sander. I want to tell everyone it's not contagious, but who even knows at this point? Maybe it is.

The doctor appears and looks to be about Willa's age. I'm squinting to read her ID tag, nodding, answering her questions. She stops talking abruptly.

"I saw you looking at my vag," she says.

"Oh my god," I say. Was I? Probably! "I'm truly the most revolting person. I'm so sorry."

"No, no, it's totally normal," she says. Is it, though? I mean sure, I guess for, like, sex offenders, gynecologists. Frat boys. She holds up her ID tag. "I'm a second-year resident. But there will be an attending present during the procedure."

Badge! Okay. Kill me.

"Oh, ha ha ha ha," I say. I am deranged! "That's fine. I think you guys might have slipped something into my drink!"

"We've added midazolam to your IV," she says. "It's a sedative." She's looking at something on her tablet. "It looks like you consented to it."

"Oh, totally!" I say. "I'm just nervous and being not at all funny by accident."

"No worries," she says.

"If only!" I say, and she leaves the room.

People start filtering in, everybody wearing scrubs now, surgical masks and booties and head coverings. I get connected to a machine that measures my vital signs; I get my armpits scanned by ultrasound to determine the "best candidate" among the many prominent lymph nodes; I am shaved, swabbed, sterilized, and injected with lidocaine. A nurse about my age takes my fingers in her own.

"I'm just going to sit here and hold your hand," she says. "You squeeze back if you need something."

"Thank you," I say. "I'll try to be brave." (Spoiler alert: I won't be.)

The attending bustles in, introduces herself with her face close to mine in a way that reassures me.

"Our residents are the best in the world, but I'm going to be here the whole time," she says. "You don't need to worry."

I nod, worried.

"You've done an axillary node?" she asks the resident quietly, over by the sink where they're washing their hands.

"No," the resident answers quietly. "But I've sat in on a

couple." I see my heart race a little on the machine then settle, and the nurse squeezes my hand. I try to look up instead, but there's a vast brown stain spread across the ceiling tiles, and Nick and I just finished a true-crime podcast series featuring a body leaking for years directly above an active office space. I look back at the machine.

The procedure starts, and it is like sitting in the back seat of your driver's ed car, listening to the instructor talk in a calm panic to the student who's mixing up the gas and the brakes and is also about to steer everybody into a ravine. "No, no," the attending says. "You have to go in at an angle. It's okay, you're doing fine. No, no. At an angle. You're going to have to bypass that nerve there. Wait, wait. That's the nerve right there. No! No! Do you have the tray? You're going to need to get the tray in there. Careful. Okay, stop. Stop. Stop! Withdraw the punch. We're going to have to try this again."

"Doing great!" she says to me, and I give a reflexive two thumbs up.

Now she's talking to the resident in an actual whisper. "Let's try a different site," she whispers. She presses the ultrasound transducer back into my armpit. "This node is a little smaller, but it's closer to the surface." I'm trying to figure out, without moving, if they've already permanently paralyzed my arm or not. This is a teaching hospital, and this is how people learn. I do understand this fact rationally. It might as well be me, right? I mean, it has to be someone. There is more whispering. "We can always do a third punch if we're not confident about the first two. Careful, careful. There's that nerve again." I can feel tears leaking into my hair, and the nurse squeezes my hand again. I picture the severed nerve, my arm dangling like a marionette's. I picture my punctured lymph node, the yuck leaking out to infect the rest of my body with a mysterious ailment. I squeeze back.

"We're getting a little tachycardia here," the nurse says, watching my heart rate go up, up, up on the machine. "I wonder if you doctors might consider trading places."

"Is that what you want?" the attending asks me neutrally. "Should I take over? It's your call."

I am fully crying now, and I hate myself for it. "I guess so," I say miserably. "I'm so sorry. I'm just scared."

The attending finishes the procedure in about one minute. Nobody speaks. The doctors close up the wound, instruct the nurse to instruct me on aftercare, and leave the room, bidding me a curt farewell as the door swings closed behind them.

"That was not on you," the nurse says.

"Thank you," I say. I'm still crying, sitting up now to put on my clothes which have appeared beside me in a plastic bag. "Thank you for rescuing me."

"You're just a living person," she says, and shakes her head. "It's not anatomy class. You're not a cadaver."

"I do kind of feel like one, though," I say.

"Of course you do," she says. "I mean, we're all cadavers, aren't we?" She laughs a laugh that has the sound of cigarettes in it, and, perversely, I want one. She opens her arms, and I lean in for the big hug she's offering.

"Just cadavers in the making," she says, and I say, "Amen."

Chapter 19

Nick is helping me undress in our room at the bed-and-breakfast where we're staying on Boston's South Shore. We're here for the Southeastern Massachusetts Magazine Awards Night, SEMMAN, which everyone pronounces *semen* in a gross way. And by *everyone* I mean the eleven people who were at the ceremony, where I did not win in the Family and Parenting category for my *Fun! Magazine* piece about twenty-five things to do with an old sock. *Fun!* had offered to book us a room for the night, and I'd thanked them, typed, *Please note that we hate inns/traditional bed-and-breakfasts*, but then felt like the kind of monster who doesn't like perching on spindly antique chairs to chitchat with strangers over dusty scones, so I deleted it and, well, here we are.

"Help yourselves to a cookie," the innkeeper said when we checked in, and she gestured to a platter with a single cookie on it. "My husband is supposed to be baking more, but he's passing a kidney stone." A muffled groan filtered in from a room behind us, and she rolled her eyes. Because she was a nasty old crone, I appreciated her on principle—but wished nonetheless that we were at an aseptic, impersonal Marriott Courtyard. We headed to our room with a gigantic metal key that has surely been used during its lifetime as an instrument of bludgeoning. "Breakfast is in the den from seven fifteen to seven forty-five," the innkeeper croaked after us. "Get there early if you're going to want any frittata. The guests here eat like pigs."

Our room smells so thickly of mothballs that it's like a substance in the air; I picture us leaving black-lunged, but—silver lining!—permanently mothproofed. Also, there's a four-poster bed with a nasty lace canopy draped over the top like a large ghost has dropped her undies here on her way up into the attic. There are many wreaths made of faded plastic flowers, many haunted wicker baskets and chairs, many admonishing signs everywhere: DON'T WASH YOUR FEET IN THE SINK! NO BANANAS IN THE TRASH! THE BED IS NOT A TRAMPOLINE! "Is the bed a trampoline?" Nick asked, testing my knowledge of the room's constraints and limitations. "Yes?" I said. He jumped on it to make me laugh, and one of the posts fell off and thudded to the ground, tangling Nick up in the ghost underpants.

But now he's unzipping my dress because I'm unable to reach up or back because of the biopsy wound/severed nerve/marionette arm.

"I can't believe I lost to that journalist who wrote about a seventh-generation family farm surviving poverty and climate catastrophe," I say, and Nick slips his hand into the sock he's just taken off and says, in a squeaky puppet voice, "There is no justice."

MAYBE I'M TOO OLD TO still be doing this magazine shit. Usually I don't, but occasionally I feel a little irrelevant. Earlier today Nick and I had popped to the beach for an hour to enjoy the clouds and the sunshine, and I'd pointed out a gorgeous old woman waist-deep in the sea, her hair streaming white behind her. "I think that's Mary Oliver," I said loudly, so he could hear me over the waves, and a kid standing nearby with a boogie board—an actual child, maybe twelve years old—shook his head pityingly, and said, "Mary Oliver's dead. That's Sharon Olds."

"AREN'T YOUR BIOPSY RESULTS SUPPOSED to come in today?" Nick squeaks.

"Okay, thank you for keeping track of that—they are, but now you need to stop with the puppet voice," I say, and Nick says, "Sorry," and pulls the sock from his hand.

"How worried are you?" he asks, and I say, "Weirdly, not that worried. They really don't think it's likely to be anything of concern." I'm climbing into my pajama bottoms. "I'm going to look at them. I am. But first I'm just going to lie down for a minute."

I use my thumb and index finger to pull back the damp yellow coverlet and climb into the damp sandy sheets, which drape and cling like they're made of human skin.

Nick, naked now, struts past, singing "Sexual Healing" and swinging his penis around, and I pat the bed, say, "Honey, honey. Shhhhh. Come and do your puzzles."

"Okay," he says agreeably. I see him start in on the Spelling Bee, which I have only become Amazing at today—the Genius category eluding me by a mere seven points. "Pangram!" he announces quickly. "Seven-pointer! *Eight*-pointer!"

"Shhhhh," I say, patting him. "You're getting a little big for your britches." He laughs.

I'm trying to read a *Boston Globe* story about the Miles Zapf case. It's from today, and so far I've read the headline twice: "New Experts Implicated in Train-Car Collision Case."

"Another eight-pointer!" Nick says. "The britches are much too small! Someone dried these britches on *hot*!"

Did you win Mama? this is a text coming in from Willa.

You're so sweet, I text. *I didn't, but I'm having a fun time with Dad in a gross and spooky inn.*

She sends me a trophy emoji, a ghost, and a heart. She must be with my dad, because a minute later he texts too. *You're always a winner*, he writes. *The best in every category.* The top of my chest burns with love. Or with garlicky salmon entrée. Something. I shake a quintet of Tums into my hand from the bottle on my bedside table.

Nick, beside me, makes a sudden triumphant bugling sound.

"What are you even doing?" I say, looking over at his phone.

"I'm sharing my Genius status with you like a braggart!" he laughs.

"You're not," I say. "You just AirDropped it to the innkeeper."

He looks at his phone. "Oh, shit, I did."

"*Oh my god, Dad*," I say, since the kids aren't here to say it.

I show Nick the Miles Zapf story on my phone. "What is this headline code for?" I ask. "Who are the experts?"

He pulls his eyebrows up toward his hairline, says, "Did you read the piece?"

"Not yet," I say. "Did you?"

"I did," he says.

"And?"

"And—you should read it."

"Why are you being weird?" I say, and Nick says, "Am I?"

"You are," I say. I'm two paragraphs in now. "Oh," I say. "Ugh. The train people retained the services of a *consulting firm*? This is going to be ugly." I picture Christine Zapf dogged by experts trying to prove her son was depressed so they can whistle all the way to the bank with the money they're not paying her. "They're going to push the suicide angle."

"No," Nick says gently. "That's not the story. The story is that they hired a consulting firm *before*. Before the accident. That's who recommended the staffing reduction, the delayed maintenance of the equipment. This is the story that's coming out now."

"Oh, ugh!" I picture a black-cloaked villain with an abacus, sliding around the beads for money and human life, balancing profit and legal fees, grief represented nowhere.

"I'm going to have to ask Jamie about it," I say. I can't believe this is the line of work our own son is in. It's so grim. "Even though Willa thinks—" Nick interrupts me, which is unusual.

"Rocky," he says. "Honey."

"What?" I say, though probably I already know. The hairs prickle on the back of my neck.

"Don't," I say, though he will. The inevitability is unfurling across me like a lead apron. I'm staring numbly at my phone, at an email that says, *You have abnormal results. Click here to view them.*

"The consulting firm," Nick says. "It's Dickens. The railroad company is Jamie's account."

Chapter 20

Nick breaks the brittle silence in the Subaru. We're driving home from the shore, and I've slept not at all and am so devastated and angry and afraid that I feel like a pustulant helium balloon no longer tied to anybody's wrist, floating up, up, and tearfully away.

"He wanted to talk to you about it in person," Nick says again, and I say again, "You should have explained that you weren't comfortable keeping a secret from me."

Nick shakes his head, presses his lips together. If we fight for too long, his switch eventually flips from remorse to anger. Maybe everybody's does. "I don't understand why you're mad at me and not Jamie," he says.

"Are you fucking *kidding* me?" I say. "You wish I were mad at *our son*?" But I *am* mad at our son.

"No, no," he says. He merges onto the highway, engages cruise control. "Of course not. I don't know. I feel like you cut the kids endless slack but you're so quick to be furious at me."

"You're not my *child*, Nick," I say to him. "You're actually not a child at all." But I look at his bewildered profile, and I think: *Of course he is. A child. Someone's child, to be treated with tenderness and care. To be loved and forgiven.*

I rest my hand on his thigh, and he moves one of his own hands from the steering wheel to cover it. If a genie swelled up out of a lamp's spout to grant him anything, I'm pretty sure Nick would pick an absence of conflict. If there were three wishes, he might pick an absence of conflict as the second one too, just to be absolutely certain. The third wish might be about ice cream or world peace or NHL lingerie. "I'm sorry," I say. "I'm sorry. I don't mean to be fighting with you. I think this is just a distraction. I should be glad you were there for Jamie. I *am* glad."

"Thank you, honey," Nick says. "I know this is awful for you."

"I mean, this is just awful, *period*," I say, rage boiling back up over the lip of my pot. "I don't think it's specific to me. It should be awful for you too."

Nick sighs. He signals to pass a car that's driving one mile per hour. Maybe it's the ghost of my mother, who used to come to a full stop on the highway while she considered her exiting options. "Yes. It is," he says. "I mean, it's a really weird situation, definitely. I feel bad for Jamie that he's caught up in something so tricky. He's really bummed."

Weird. Tricky. Bummed. "We're not talking about the corner store being out of Reese's Pieces," I say. "How were you, ugh—just, like, Marvin Gaye–ing around our room all night? Someone's child is dead." I picture the clay mother, her features stretched—obliterated by grief—and I stab at my furious wet eyes with the bottom of my T-shirt.

"Yes," Nick says crisply. "And that's very sad. But, I'm sorry, Rock, it's not like our son *killed* him. Jamie's on a team that was hired to assess risk, and they did."

"I know," I say. "But, Nicky—" A sob bursts out from my face. "Jamie decided that human life was less important than people getting rich."

"Does that sound like Jamie?" Nick says, and I admit, crying some more, that it doesn't. "So let's wait and talk to him when he's here next week." He pushes a disc into the CD player, and it's Shawn Colvin, *Steady On*, from thirty-five years ago—the year we met. I understand that this is a peace offering as well as a bid to stop me from continuing to rail at him, and I accept both, wipe my face with a tissue, and return to the baffling pathology results in my portal.

Based on the core biopsy samples, the lymph node has been deemed *diffusely abnormal*, which should definitely be my stripper name. I google all the terms: *lymphocytes* and *histiocytes*, *reactive lymphoid hyperplasia* and *tingible body microphages*. There's good news and bad news, it seems, but I'm not entirely sure which is which. The final pathologic diagnosis is *indeterminate*, and there is a recommendation to schedule a spiral CT *to assess for solid tumors and granulomatous disease process in organs*. This is frightening, and I read it out loud to Nick.

"I don't love *solid tumors*," I say. "I mean, I don't love *granulomatous disease process in organs* either, but *solid tumors* is my least favorite." If he describes these results as *tricky* or *weird* or *a bummer*, I will surely murder him with the gigantic key I forgot to return to the innkeeper and now need to FedEx from home.

"Ugh," Nick says. "That's worrying."

"It is," I say.

"Don't they sometimes use the word *tumors* in a sense that's not, like, the cancer one?"

"Maybe?" I say. "I don't know. I'm getting a cancer vibe from the way it's used here."

"But if it were cancer, wouldn't they see, like, *cancer* cells?"

"I don't know," I say.

"I guess we'll schedule the CAT scan and see what they say," he says, and I wipe my leaky face some more and say, in Chicken's voice, "But cats *hate* to be scanned!"

Remember the world from back when you couldn't even find out if you had strep throat without a doctor calling the wall phone in your kitchen? Now you just click into your computer and discover that you have cancer or that you have—I'm seeing this only now—a white-blood-cell disorder called *leukopenia* or that they've scheduled your autopsy.

I put my socked feet up on the dash so I can tug my jeans away from my legs and study the rash. If I were in middle school, the bullies would nickname me "Pizza Shin." *What are you trying to tell me?* I think to the rash. *What are you?* But I know what it is. It's *me*.

Chapter 21

I'm propped up in bed with pillows and cats and a novel I keep reading the same single paragraph of, and Willa is asleep beside me. She's got the hot water bottle pressed against her stomach, the trick-or-treat bucket on the floor, and, on the bedside table, a glass of Coke and melted ice, an untouched muffin on a plate, the aromatherapy diffuser misting out the trademarked lavender-basil scent of an oil blend called Anxieteze, and a translucent orange bottle with today's date on its label and two out of three benzodiazepine tablets still inside. Music is playing softly—a Spotify mix of Willa's called "Sad Girlie Bedtime," which seems to be mostly Gracie Abrams. When Nick peeks in I make such frantic shushing noises and agitated hand gestures that you'd think we were hiding silently in the basement during a home invasion. He waves, retreats. The sun is setting into the bright maple trees, filling our room with amber light.

My sole purpose in life had become keeping the Jamie news from Willa, but I was doomed to failure. In a follow-up story about the freight company RCX and the way they'd assessed risk, the *New York Times* has finally named the consulting company. I'd been making maple-pumpkin muffins when Willa burst into the kitchen from outside, her phone held angrily aloft. "It's fucking *Dickens!*" she shouted over the noise of the mixer. "Those motherfuckers." I turned off the mixer, wiped my hands on a dish towel, and went to her. "Ugh," she said. Her eyes glittered with rage. "Of course it's all about maximizing profit. Jamie must be so angry and frustrated right now."

"I'm sure he is," I said carefully. "But, honey, that's what consulting firms *are*. That's what they do."

We were standing by the doorway, and I helped her off with her backpack, her down vest, like she was a little girl. She went to the sink and angrily filled a mason jar with water, drank it, wiped her mouth with the back of her hand. I watched her.

"But Jamie only does the kind of work they do that's"—she looked puzzled for a second—"not *that*."

I nodded, tipped my head side to side. *Maybe, maybe, not really, no.*

"Well, he wasn't part of this anyway," she said, with a confidence that made my hands tingle unpleasantly. I stretched my fingers. Maybe the solid tumors were acting up. "I mean, he couldn't have been. It would have been a conflict of interest, right? Since he knew Miles from high school."

She was standing at the sink still, and I was leaning against the butcher-block cart we call the *island*, looking at her. In a science fiction movie, I would have fast-forwarded a day and tased this scene from her memory—taken it away and left a bright coin in its place, like the tooth fairy.

When I didn't say anything Willa said, "Shit." She put the jar down so hard I wondered if it would crack. "It wouldn't have been a conflict of interest. That's why you're looking at me like that. Fuck. Because the consulting happened *before* the accident. Mama . . ." She looked the way a person looks before they blow apart into smithereens.

"Honey," I said. There was a smell like burning hair, and I remembered the pecans I was toasting in the oven. I pulled out the pan of black nuts, turned on the range hood to clear the air.

"*Jamie* did that?" Willa said, above the noise of the clattery fan. "Advised them not to deal with their safety equipment? That was *Jamie*?"

"No, no," I said. "I mean, it wasn't just Jamie. It was a team of people. I don't really know. I haven't talked to him. Dad did. But yeah, it was one of Jamie's accounts, the railroad people."

The color drained from Willa's face—like a pale gray shade pulled down over a window—and she bent over and threw up a clear puddle onto the tile floor.

"Oh!" I said. "Honey. I think we should wait and see what—"

"I'm sorry," she said. "I can't . . ." She straightened up and ran out of the kitchen and I heard the bathroom door slam behind her. I followed, put a quiet palm to the door frame, listened to the water run, the toilet flush, the sounds of Willa crying and retching.

"Honey," I called in, and she yelled, "Go away. Mama, I'm sorry. Please." The blankness of that closed door—like a portal to misery, snapped shut behind her. No access.

I returned to the kitchen and knelt with a roll of paper towels, wiped the floor. I washed and dried my hands, turned the mixer back on, sifted flour and spices, toasted a fresh batch of pecans, greased the muffin tin. I used an ice-cream scoop to portion out the fragrant batter, then I put the pan in the oven, set a timer, and returned to the bathroom door. I could hear the shower running now, the sounds of Willa sobbing. I sat on the kitchen couch, from which I could see both the oven and the bathroom door. I was an antenna attuned to my daughter's unhappiness: I could hear tissues pulled from the box, the tap turned on and off, the sound of vomiting, crying. I could hear her blink and swallow. It was vibrational. It was supernatural. It was empathy, but pathological—not just feeling what it was like to be her, but actually feeling her feelings, my heart pulled up into my throat. It was tidal, magnetic. It was extrasensory.

While Willa suffered, the house slowly filled with a warm cloud of nutmeg and clove. I was Philippe Petit, walking the wire between the Twin Towers. Or maybe I was the wire.

Willa knows about Dickens, I texted Nick. *She is completely decompensating. Barfing, crying, falling totally apart.*

I'm coming home, he texted back. *After this client. 45 minutes. Could Davey be helpful?*

When the timer rang, I pulled the muffins from the oven and toothpicked one, then tipped them all out onto a cooling rack. I sat on the couch again. Then I called Davey, Jo's husband, who picked up after the first ring. He's an emergency department doctor, and has been on high alert as our on-call physician ever since my dad moved in.

"Hey," I said. "I think Willa's having some kind of panic attack. She's been in the bathroom crying and throwing up for an hour."

"Shit, Rocky," he said. "Are you pretty sure it's not a bug?"

"Pretty sure," I said. A sob caught in my throat. "I can't stand to tell you about it, though."

"That's okay," he said. "Do you want me to talk to her?"

I held the phone in one hand and knocked softly with the other. "Hey, honey," I called through the door. "Do you want to talk to Davey?" Willa was still crying. "Honey?"

"Maybe put me on speakerphone," Davey said, and I did. I held the phone to the door.

"Hey, Willa, it's me," he said. "I'm so sorry you're having such a bad time. Do you want to tell me what's happening in your body?"

She coughed, took a shuddering breath. "I don't know, Davey," she said, crying. "I feel like I'm not going to be able to talk to you."

"That's okay," he said. "You're going through something. You don't have to talk to me." This is not the first time Davey has coached Willa through this kind of anxiety—the kind that sinks its teeth into her neck and will not release her.

Willa was breathing more quietly, still crying. "I feel it in my throat," she said. "In my stomach."

"Okay, yeah," Davey said. "That makes sense. Your body is giving you information about what's happening in your brain. It's another way you're feeling your hard feelings. Do you want to call your therapist? What's his name—Dr. Slinkypants?"

"No," she said, crying and laughing a little. "I mean, I will? I just don't want to right now. I can't."

"That's okay," Davey said. "You're just moving through this, and your mom is there with you."

"Yeah," she said.

"There's a big, wide net of people who adore you. We've got you. I know you know that."

"Yeah," she said again.

"Do you think you'd be able to sleep?" he said, and she said no. "Do you still have the Ativan from your primary care doc—it might have been from last year?" Willa said she didn't have it or she didn't know where it was if she did. "Okay," Davey said. "I'm going to call in a prescription for you. Just something so you can sleep, and it will take the edge off the nausea too. Okay?"

"Okay," she said in a tiny voice. "Thank you, Davey." And he said of course, and that he loved her, and that this day would be only one chapter in the long book of her life.

By the time I got back from the pharmacy, Willa was in my bed, wrapped in a bath towel and curled up on her side. I handed her a pill and a glass of water, and she sat up a little to sip and swallow. I set up the diffuser and the speaker. I brought the cats in and pushed them under the covers to make them stay. I crept downstairs to get her a muffin and a glass of Coke, but when I came back up she was crying again.

I sat on the edge of the mattress and rubbed small circles between her shoulder blades, her skin as smooth as a dolphin's.

"Jamie's my favorite," she said. "He's the actual best. Do I get to keep feeling like that?"

"Of course," I said immediately, and she scoured my face with her eyes. *Why "of course"?*

"But Miles Zapf is permanently dead," she said. "There's not a way that this just, like, turns out to be fine. I can't see the path to . . ." She paused then, but I understood. *To us being okay.*

I SHOULD HAVE WORRIED WHEN Willa was a toddler. I did worry. She was the most passionate person I had ever met: she sobbed when she couldn't pull her own fingers off like they were gloves; she lay down on her back on the sidewalk like a bag of furious gravel when I scolded her for running out into the street; she pressed her forehead affectionately to mine, but so forcefully she was like a demented battering ram, bruising me with love.

"JAMIE WILL BE UP ON Friday. Do you want to wait until he's here? It might be easier to understand everything when he's right here, just being Jamie." I was talking to myself as much as to her, of course. Willa nodded and closed her eyes, then snapped them open, then closed them again.

To have a child is to have your heart go walking around outside your body for the rest of your life—so the saying goes. Not a pink bubble of a heart, but the bloodied organ itself, dragged through the gutter behind a team of wild horses, returned to you in tatters if at all. The urge to flee is strong. I picture *Runaway Bunny*, the mama rabbit promising to follow her baby wherever it goes—only the opposite. If this bedroom window opened and a ladder appeared, I would climb down and away. I would become a trout, a crocus. I would become a rock in the mountain high above, and my children would become mountain climbers to climb to me, but I would still be a rock.

Now Willa's breathing evens out and she is finally asleep. *Love you*, Jo has texted. *Being a parent is unsurvivable. It's the movie Poltergeist every second.* I picture the impossibility of retrieving your child from inside a malevolent TV; I picture a weird pumpkin thing opening up in the wall and sucking everybody into its horrible guts; I picture the family home built over a graveyard. *Exactly*, I write, then creep back downstairs, flipping lights on as I go. I find my dad on the kitchen couch eating a muffin.

"These are delicious," he says. "This is my second one. They're very, very good."

"Thanks, Dad," I say, and when I burst into tears, he says, "Oh, Rachel." He makes a space for me beside him and rubs my back while I cry into my hands, comforting me the way my mom would have, even though he's still chewing, crumbs showering down around us.

"I could live without the nuts," he says, and I say, "Noted."

Chapter 22

The editor has assigned me one final spatchcocking sidebar—about brining versus dry salting—and I should be trying to finish it before Jamie and Maya arrive. But I'm not. Instead, I'm simmering lentils in a slow cooker full of wine and herbs. I've baked a huge pan of rosemary-scented focaccia. And I've made up the guest bed with fresh sheets, put a jar full of lilacs on the dresser in there. I'd been refusing to enjoy the lilacs on principle—it's October, for fuck's sake!—until Willa called me out. "It's climate change and it's bad, whether or not you enjoy the off-season lilacs," she said. "So you might as well enjoy the lilacs." This seemed like a sensible enough point.

Now I'm cleaning the bathroom, using a coat hanger to fish from the drain a raccoon-sized clump of my own hair. Angie is sitting on my back while I bend over the tub, and she growls at the clump when it emerges. Chicken, standing beside us on the bath mat, jumps in fright and scrabbles out of the room. Hair loss is either a side effect of the methotrexate, a symptom of the illness itself, or some combination. What better way to accessorize a fancy floor-length rash than with patchy baldness! When I inspect my hairline in the mirror, I notice a couple of bumps on my forehead that aren't moles or acne. Until now my face has been surprisingly, happily unaffected—but there, above my right eyebrow, are two pearly lumps and a dime-sized purple smudge. Thanks for nothing, methotrexate! So far all the medication seems to be accomplishing is heartburn, headaches, and hair so thin I could cinch my ponytail with this ten-year-old braces rubber band I find at the bottom of the toothbrush cup.

Still, I take the medicine weekly, obediently, and although I started with four pills, the goal is to ramp up to twelve over a couple of months by increasing my dose two pills every two weeks. But first I need to get blood work to ascertain that my liver is handling the medication okay. And then, after the results confirm this, the doctor needs to call in a new prescription, since I only get exactly two weeks of the medication at a time. They won't call in the blood work until it's been exactly two weeks since I last got it. So, in one single day, these things need to happen: I need to remind them to call in the blood work; they need to call in the blood work; I need to go to the lab to get the blood work done; I need to check my portal for the results; I need to let the practice know the results look okay; I need to remind them to call in the new prescription; I need to pick up the medication and take it, since it's imperative that I take it on the same day every week.

This is not what happens.

This is what happens: I get to the lab and there are no blood-work orders. Or they run the wrong series of tests. Or nobody checks to see either the results or my message that the results are in. Or the pharmacy hasn't gotten approval from my insurance company for the new prescription. Or the prescription is for the wrong dose. Or the pharmacy is out of the medication altogether. "I'm so sorry to trouble you . . ." I say into the phone. *Ugh, sorry, me again!* I write in the portal. "Could you possibly . . . ?" I say from the kitchen floor, where I'm lying in a pool of blood because it's like a game of Whac-A-Mole, only there aren't any moles, so you might as well use the mallet to bludgeon yourself to death. Set yourself on fire afterward for good measure, so you can rise from your own ashes to yell, *Talk to a pharmacist!* at the appropriate prompt. *That option is unavailable. To return to the main menu, press 4.*

Now I'm tossing dirty things in a laundry basket as I clean, including an inexplicable number of regular washcloths and some tiny washcloths that belong to Willa's American Girl dolls. Is she using them herself? Or is she wiping her dolls' dirty little faces? Who knows. She still gets the American Girl catalogues, still studies them like scripture. Actually, thanks to those catalogues, Willa was recently able identify an odd and spindly piece of furniture in a neighbor's driveway. It had a FREE sign on it.

"The price is right—but what would you do with it?" I said.

"It's called a *whatnot*," she said, confidently. "Rebecca Rubin has one—she's the Jewish American Girl doll."

I looked at her. "Do we need one?" I said. "Is that where we should be keeping our yarmulkes and gefilte fish and *whatnot?*" But Willa was examining it in earnest.

"Do you think this would fit in my room?" she said, and I said no.

Now I bring the laundry basket around to the shack, only my dad doesn't seem to be there. I knock on the door, call in. "Dad! It's me! Do you have any laundry?" When he doesn't answer, I open the door a crack and call in again before stepping inside. The place is immaculate, as always, and it smells good—like coffee and oranges and Old Spice. I'm briefly relieved before I hear my dad groaning from the bedroom. He's sitting up against the pillows when I rush in, and his cheeks are a little pink, but he looks more or less fine. My mom's side of the bed is still neatly made, the way it always is.

"You scared me!" I say, and he says, "I have a head cold." His voice sounds wet and thick.

"Oh no, Dad, I'm so sorry." He shrugs, coughs into a handkerchief.

"It is what it is," he says. "But my temperature is eighty degrees, which seems low."

"Indeed," I say. I make a mental note to replace his thermometer, which is doubtless from the 1960s and the mercury all leaked out into somebody's butthole decades ago. Probably my own! That might explain a lot, actually.

"I'll want to do a Covid test," I say. I am remembering that my immune system is being suppressed and I should be wearing a mask—but I don't want to get into it with my dad. I turn my head to the side to inhale, because I assume the air is cleaner six inches to my left, ha ha ha. Kill me.

My dad, meanwhile, is pish-poshing his irritated hand through the air. "It's not Covid," he says. "It's from this stupid air conditioner." He gestures at the window unit, which we bought just this past spring.

"Like, black mold?" I say, and he says, "No! Not mold. A cold. When it was hot the other afternoon, I turned the air conditioner on and I knew from the way it was blowing on my neck that it was going to give me a cold." When I open my mouth to speak, he interrupts me. "Don't tell me I can't get a cold from the air conditioner. I know it's fallen out of fashion, but I'm telling you. That's what happened."

I think about Laura Ingalls Wilder's family mistaking their malaria for a bad case of Eating Very Cold Watermelon. But then again, I have an entire team of doctors with no idea what I've got or where it came from. Maybe my dad's right.

"Okay," I say. "What can I get you? Chicken soup? A poached egg? Tea? Cough medicine?"

"I took this." He reaches around on his bedside table and hands me a brown glass bottle that looks like it might have washed up on shore with a message in it from the *Lusitania*.

"'Elixir of terpin hydrate with codeine,'" I read from the faded label. "Wow, Dad! Talk about things that have fallen out of fashion. Are you feeling very, very relaxed?"

"Pretty relaxed," he says, and laughs.

I'm sitting on the side of his bed now, googling. "You missed out. Apparently you could have gotten terpin hydrate with *heroin*," I say. "Oh, but that was only in 1907."

"Alas," my dad says.

"You brought, like, one suitcase when you came up here. You packed *this*?"

He shrugs again. "Mom always gave me a spoonful if I was under the weather."

Two people shared a single bottle of cough medicine for fifty-eight years, and it's still a third full. I can't help feeling a pang of envy. Why didn't I inherit their old-world robustness?

"That reminds me," he says. "I found this in my dopp kit."

He reaches around on the bedside table again, hands me an ancient plastic bottle.

"I don't know if it will help," he says shyly. "I didn't want to draw attention." He gestures at the cuff of my sweatshirt, at my blotchy, crusty wrist.

I shake the bottle—watch the clear top layer swirl into the pink sludge below. It's calamine lotion.

"Thanks, Dad," I manage to say, and he says, "You're welcome."

Chapter 23

Nick, Willa, and I are leaning against our car in the dark, waiting for Jamie at the train station. It's the train he always catches after work, which means he'll get in close to midnight. It's a tradition—all of us piling into the car to go get him—and we're always excited.

We've already gotten a slightly cryptic text that Maya's not coming. *She's good, she's fine*, Jamie wrote after I responded with alarm. *The cephalopods are proving v demanding.* Maya is employed by the Museum of Natural History, where, until recently, she was the invertebrate collections manager. Now that she's finished her paleontology PhD she's been promoted to director of ocean life, and she works long hours. She's putting together a huge exhibit of the five-hundred-million-year-long evolution of the octopus, which Nick has suggested she name "Squid Marks."

"I guess I just want to agree now that we won't make Jamie feel like it's an inquisition into his decency," I'm saying. "Or, like, an intervention about his principles. It's just us. He's not on trial." When nobody speaks, I lean out to look at their faces, and Nick and Willa both have the exact same expression of bemused irritation. "I'm the only one who would make him feel like that?"

I say, and they nod. I lean back against the car. "That's probably true," I say. "Note to self."

Oh! But here it is! The whistle of the train approaching. It always makes me think of *Owl Moon*, a book we read to the kids when they were little: *Somewhere behind us a train whistle blew, long and low, like a sad, sad song.* The lines catch in the throat of my mind now, the train's song sadder than ever, even as we move toward the door, the three of us. People are streaming from the station, and here he is rushing toward us, into our arms, our smiley, beautiful boy, with his hair still falling over his forehead, his eyes crinkled up with joy. "Hi! Hi!" we are all saying, and it's him—it's just him. Still him. It's Jamie.

My arms are folded around him, my face pressed into his shoulder, and he smells rich—like evergreen and tonka beans and money and also, beneath that, the way he's always smelled: his baby scalp, his milky breath, the skin of his cheeks as rosy and taut as a nectarine even though he's got a five-o'clock shadow now too.

"Is this leather?" Willa asks, butching the suitcase out of his hands to load it into the car, and when he says it is, she says, "Dude," and shakes her head in disgust or admiration.

On the drive home, we ask all the usual things, and he answers: His trip was good, easy. There was just a single delay outside of New Haven. He ate a sandwich from the fancy Italian deli near Penn Station—something called "L'Inferno" that's porchetta and grilled peppers and arugula on ciabatta. Actually, he still has half in his bag if anybody wants. Nick does, and drives with one hand while he eats, groaning with the deliciousness.

"That truffle mayo hits so hard," he says, and I say, "I thought you hated truffle."

Nick shrugs. "I'm changing," he says. "Don't fence me in."

The kids are in the back together, like always, and I have my automatic heart-swollen all-is-right-with-the-world feeling, even though so much is wrong with the world—the world in general and ours in particular. "Hey, Will, thanks for your text," I hear Jamie say quietly, and she says quietly back, "Oh! Of course. Thank you for yours."

"How was your date with Weird Al Yankovic's daughter's ex-girlfriend?" Jamie asks her, proving for the zillionth time that I know nothing about anything, and Willa sighs. "Kinda mid. If there's no chemistry apple picking, there's really not going to be any chemistry," she says, and Jamie agrees, sings a few bars of "Amish Paradise," interrupts himself to ask after their grandfather.

"He's good in general," I say. "Though he's got a little cold right now. Honestly, you'd think it was a complicated case of smallpox, the amount of kvetching—"

"Yikes, Mama," Jamie interrupts. "I mean, he's ninety-two years old. Should we be taking him to the hospital?"

"That's what I said!" Willa says.

"No, no," I say. "It's nothing like that. He's just got a cold. He got it from the air conditioner somehow, because maybe he's, like, an HVAC cyborg and they share some of the same DNA? He's really okay. Go back there tomorrow and see for yourself—actually, please do, he's excited to see you. But really, he's fine. He'll outlive us all." Willa and I both knock on the side of the car, and I say, "Sorry, sorry." We are too superstitious for such frivolous optimism.

Jamie asks Willa about her fruit flies, and Willa complains that they've mutated and now their brains are not bioluminescing the way they're supposed to. *Same*, I think to say, but don't.

Nobody asks Jamie about his work.

When we pull into the driveway and tumble out under the stars, Jamie wonders if we want to take a night walk.

"It's one in the morning!" I say, and Jamie laughs and says, "Luckily you're already in your pajamas." Am I? I look down. I am! I read somewhere that young people are night owls because they're the strongest members of any given clan: they evolved to watch over the rest of us while we're sleeping. I picture muscled cave youth with their bone hair ornaments, sitting alertly by the fire with clubs and massive rocks. I picture my own kids, stoned and rewatching the Bad Bunny Tiny Desk Concert, directing whoever came along up the stairs to assault Nick and me in our bed.

"Okay," I say. "I'm in."

We head into the woods, and the moon is bright enough that nobody needs Nick to turn on his flashlight, though he offers. It's single file for a while, and we barely talk, mostly just alerting each other to roots and stumps, until we fall out of the forest into the fields behind the neighboring farm, where we can walk four abreast. The moon is low and bright in the sky, and we can see the black shapes of a row of dahlias hit by early frost. "It smells so good," Jamie says. "The leaves." Willa slings her arm around my shoulder. We all stop walking when Jamie does. He inhales, exhales, inhales again, shakes his head, and says, "I was worried about this exact kind of thing." There will be no preamble. Here we go.

"We know you were, honey," I say, and it's true. He had been.

"The headhunter—" he starts, and it is never not jarring to me, that term. Was Jamie the one hunting? No, no. He'd been hunted. I picture *Heart of Darkness*, and Jamie is Charles Marlow looking for Kurtz, and also he is Kurtz. He is the Martin Sheen character in *Apocalypse Now*, and he is Marlon Brando mumbling in his cave, surrounded by decapitation.

"—he said that Dickens would let you identify industries you weren't comfortable working in," Jamie continues. "And I was like, *Great!* You guys remember." We do. It was a relief at the time—that Jamie could say *no* to tobacco, Big Pharma, weapons. "But now I'm not totally sure how much of a difference it makes," he's saying. "I mean, yeah, it's not OxyContin or bombs, it's the railroad—and that sounded so fun to me! In a picture-book way. Remember how I always wanted to take an overnight train?" We do. "But then it's all kind of the same thing. We're increasing shareholder profits. That's what we get hired to do. There are always going to be costs and compromises. Acceptable risk. I could be working in a jelly bean factory, and we'd be calculating the acceptable number of workers who could fall into the boiling syrup, the acceptable number of kids who could choke and die on Easter morning." He sounds more weary than anything else. "I love the work, but it's a pretty disappointing mission."

Miles Zapf's unspoken name hangs invisibly in the cold air, even though the word *disappointing* is a conspicuous puff of white. The breeze is picking up now, blowing through my pajama bottoms, and I unwrap Willa's arm from me so I can lean into Nick. "Um, excuse me," she says, "I was still using that." She wriggles between us and pulls my arm back around her. The leaves are whispering all around.

"The thing is," Jamie says. "RCX—they'd basically already decided what they were going to do. Outsourcing maintenance to nonunion workers, deferring repairs—all of it. They came to us with those ideas." He stops talking to chew on his cuticle, which is not a habit of his I'm familiar with. "They were going to save ten million dollars, and they paid us a million to say their own plan back to them. To, like, make it into a slide deck." He shrugs. "I mean, it is what it is." *What is it?* I don't ask. "Even if RCX is responsible for"—he hesitates—"the death, and it's not totally clear to me that they are, that was the kind of risk already built into the calculation."

I disentangle myself from the huddle so I can see Willa's face, which is strangely blank. Her moral compass is usually inviolable, but Jamie's magnetism is creating some kind of interference.

"Your calculation?" I say. "Or theirs?" My voice sounds thin to me, maybe because I hadn't planned on speaking. I am happy not to hear myself ask when exactly it was that he drank the Kool-Aid. *It's Jamie*, I keep thinking, like a mantra. *It's our Jamie.*

He shakes his head. "Theirs, I guess," he says without conviction. I take two steps toward him and wrap an arm around his waist.

"Ugh," I say, because it's either the one *ugh* or a flood of words, some of which I'll inevitably regret. I hear something that might be an owl, but when I listen for it, I don't hear it again. *Sometimes there's an owl and sometimes there isn't.*

"I really feel like we should go back to the house and make nachos," Nick says, and Jamie laughs.

"That's the most Dad suggestion ever," he says. He's squinting toward the edge of the farm, where the black tree silhouettes look like the backdrop of a puppet theater. He points. "Why is it so green back there?" Everyone turns to look. "And purple. Oh my god, you guys! Is that the northern lights?"

"Holy fuck!" Willa says. "It's totally the northern lights. Oh my fucking god, are we in *Iceland*? What the actual *fuck*?"

"So much profanity," I say, and Willa gives me the finger.

We've heard you can see the colors better through your phone camera, and it's true. My phone's back at the house, so I look on with Willa, who says, "Is it cheating, though—looking through your phone?"

"It's not cheating," Jamie says. "It's amplifying beauty. That's just human impulse." I think of picture frames, binoculars, lipstick. He's right.

We will go in and make nachos—we will. In just a few minutes we'll be warm again, microwaving cheddar on chips, spooning out sour cream and pickled rings of jalapeno. But first there's this: a shimmering, shifting curtain of pink and green as particles from the sun collide, as they hit the Earth's atmosphere at unimaginable speeds. Now it's a swirl, now a funnel. The stars glitter above us in a regular way, but the clouds iridesce and scud off. Our little family stands still while the lights storm, pointing here and there, exclaiming. It's breathtaking; it's magic; it's completely unreal. Aurora borealis. And we're not in any danger, of course. But that's not exactly how it feels.

Chapter 24

Nick is making his famous brown-butter waffles, the yeasty batter steaming in the hot iron, sending clouds of intoxicating aroma into all corners of the house. The kitchen is brightly sunlit, and I've set our wooden table with big white plates and faded cloth napkins, put out butter and syrup, mason jars of jam and jelly. There's a white pitcher of late-blooming pink cosmos and a blue bowl heaped with clementines. I'm frying bacon on the griddle, pressing it flat with tongs so it cooks evenly. Willa floats in sleepily, like a cartoon character hypnotized by a good smell.

"Mmmm," she says, sitting heavily on the kitchen couch. "I was hoping there'd be waffles. What can I do to help?" She's already stretching out her legs, pulling a blanket up over herself.

"Do you want to fill water glasses?" I say, and she laughs, says, "No."

Angie leaps onto her from somewhere, and Willa cries, "Uh-oh! Special delivery from Tiny Town!" and wraps her up in the blanket. I can hear her purring from where I'm standing at the stove, even with the fan on. "I thought I ordered a bigger one," Willa scolds the kitten. "This one has a too-small head."

The bacon is all crisped and laid out on a platter of paper

towels, and I'm filling water glasses when the door opens and my dad shuffles in in his slippers.

"Grandpa!" Willa says, and he says, "You're surprised? You thought I'd have died in the night?" She laughs.

I dry my hands on my apron, kiss his cheek. "How are you feeling? You sound so much better. I wasn't sure we'd see you for breakfast."

"I feel a lot better. I took half a Valium, which seems to have done the trick. That and the Chessmen cookies." If I live to be ninety, I too will scatter my curative folk wisdom all over the place. Also, how does Pepperidge Farm keep making those cookies? I am under the impression that my dad is their sole consumer.

"Hello, Grandson," my dad is saying, and there's Jamie in the doorway, rumpled and boyish in a gray hoodie and red flannel pajama bottoms.

"Hello, Grandfather," Jamie says, wrapping his long arms around my dad's back.

"I know you're working hard, but you look good," my dad says.

"Thanks, Grandpa," Jamie says. "You too." My dad rolls his eyes.

The first round of waffles is ready, and Nick beckons everyone to the table, where he's presiding over the iron.

"Let me sit this round out," I say. Each waffle only makes four squares.

My dad looks at me. "Are you all right, Rachel?" he asks without sarcasm, and I say, "Of course."

"Mama's not eating gluten," Willa explains to Jamie. This

is not anything I've actually shared aloud, but it's true. I've put myself on something called the OSIS Diet. Or maybe it's called the ITIS Diet? I don't even think it stands for anything—aside from the fact that you have an unpronounceable disease that ends with a pathological suffix. The diet is supposed to be anti-inflammatory, and it's too dull to talk about, since it's everything you already knew you should be eating, e.g., kale. Wake me when the Buttered Rye Toast Diet is a thing.

"I'm not *not* eating gluten," I say.

"Are you eating gluten?" Willa says, and I say, "Not really, no."

"Coffee?" my dad says. "Please?"

"Oh, shit," I say. "Yes. I made some. It's in the carafe." Nick stands to get it, grabs mugs out of the cupboard, pulls the half-and-half from the fridge.

"Can you please pass me whatever that is?" Willa points to a jar that has an inch of pinkish jam left in it. "It's because of her weird rash," she explains to Jamie.

"What weird rash?" Jamie says. He stops spraying whipped cream out of the can, looks at me, and says, "Oh, I see it, Mama. On your wrists? That?"

"Yes," I say.

"Oh my god, no," Willa says. "It's everywhere. Like, all over her entire body. She's not drinking alcohol either."

"Wait," Jamie says. "You're not drinking alcohol?" Jamie is my favorite person to drink with, so this is sad news all around. Maya doesn't really drink. Nick doesn't drink much either, or Willa. Who is he going to shake up a mai tai for? I mean, my dad, maybe. But who is going to sit around the Hell's Kitchen bars with him, ordering opaquely golden pints of piney beer?

I love to drink! How could I be not drinking? I hadn't even known it was true—not exactly—until I hear Willa say it.

"Luckily it's Mama, so she can get stoned from, like, the enoki garnish on her gluten-free ramen," Willa says, and Jamie laughs.

My dad holds out his hand and Willa passes him the jam jar. He takes his glasses off to read the label and says to me, "Did Mom make this?"

"If it's gooseberry, then yes," I say.

"It's gooseberry," he says, the rims of his eyes reddening. "I don't like gooseberries." He pronounces it *gooze-breeze*, the way she did. "But I miss Grandma." We all do. She should be here daintily cutting her waffle into tidy bites with a knife and fork instead of picking it up and folding it in her gorilla hands like the rest of us. She should be here to witness our joy and our sorrow.

"Why aren't you drinking?" Jamie asks. He's peeling a clementine now while he waits for the next round of waffles.

"Oh, I don't know," I say. "I mean, it's turning out that alcohol's not quite the cure-all we thought it was."

When I talked to the Boston rheumatologist before the spiral CT, she said, "Look, Rocky. You're fifty-five years old. The CT will spot something—it just will. I want you to understand that fact going in. Whatever we see—it may or may not be relevant to the rash, the blood work. Try not to worry too much." This was good advice, theoretically speaking. Because while the scan located no evidence of solid tumors, it has made an anomalous finding in my liver. Specifically, the radiologist has noted *multifocal subsegmental intrahepatic biliary ductal dilatation of uncertain etiology*. Anyone who cut and pasted that repulsive set of words into Google would stop drinking in a cold-turkey fright. A follow-up MRI has been recommended, along with a screening for ulcerative colitis and something called a *fluid thrill test*, which sounds like a nineties alternative rock band named after an amusement park ride. I have scheduled both procedures, and, in the event, I *am* worrying too much!

"Edith had gallbladder surgery," my dad says, apropos of nothing, about one of his old bridge partners.

"Oh," I say, and he shakes his head.

"I'm sorry," he says. "Scratch that. It's really not going to be a conversation worth having." My parents used to call this style of chitchat the *organ recital*. It was primarily abdominal in nature, although you could also discuss detached retinas, cataracts, floaters, and anything else ophthalmic, as well as such podiatric woes such as corns and bunions. I feel like I'm going to be a little early to the organ recital, which is too bad.

The waffle iron beeps, and Nick distributes the squares, holds one up and raises his eyebrows to me. I shake my head, take another strip of bacon, which is not technically OSIS or ITIS, but fuck it.

"Jamie, am I right that your company is involved in this train accident?" my dad says, and Jamie looks up from the plate he's flooding with syrup and says, "You are. I mean, we were involved before. It's not work that's ongoing."

My dad nods. "Dickens has also done some consulting for the Federal Railroad Administration, is that right?"

Jamie wipes his mouth with a napkin. His face, usually clear as a bell, clouds over with something that might be wariness.

Or dread. "That's right, Grandpa. That wasn't my account, but yes."

"Wait, what?" Willa says. Her plate is a chaos of jam and whipped cream, and I can only assume there's a waffle somewhere beneath. "What does that mean?"

Jamie sighs. This is the boy who used to warn you that he felt a *stripe-tastic feeling* coming on before covering a piece of paper with exuberantly painted lines of pink and purple. He used to wake Willa for school with a made-up call-and-response song that ended with the lines *I hope you're feeling happy! Cuz I'm happy too!* Even Willa, whose morning personality was more spitting cobra than human child, was floated aloft on his buoyancy. He chose not to write a thesis in college—those bong hits were not going to smoke themselves, was the vibe we got—but the economics department awarded him a prize anyway. We suspected they'd invented it just for him. It was called something like the John Maynard Keynes Sunshine Award for Good Cheer, and it came with a check for two hundred dollars. "It's always fun to privilege the privileged," Willa snarked, and this was fair. But she wants everything for him in spite of herself. I do too, of course. And god knows, we all make bad decisions sometimes. But have we mistaken Jamie's good nature for goodness?

No, no. Of course not. That's a crazy question. I'm ashamed to have allowed it to flit past, even during this season of doubt.

What do I know? How can I be sure I know it? I realize I am not the first skeptic to wonder.

"There are lots of different companies and agencies who own different parts of the rail system," Jamie is explaining now.

"And the Federal Railroad Administration—they're kind of an umbrella government agency in charge of regulation and safety. Oversight."

"That's weird," Willa says, and Jamie says, "What is?"

"That *oversight* means paying attention and also not paying attention."

"That *is* weird," Jamie says.

"But that feels kind of sleazy, right?" Willa says. "Dickens advising both of them?"

Jamie tips his head right to left. "I mean, yes and no," he says. "It's different teams making different kinds of recommendations in terms of efficiency. I don't really know anything about the company's work with the FRA."

I want to ask if *efficiency* is just code for laying everybody off and risking people's lives. I want to ask how they quantified the death of a kid. What was it worth in their calculations, Miles Zapf's life? In an interview, I saw one of the freight executives refer to his "life-changing injuries." I bite my tongue.

The waffle iron dings again, and nobody moves, except Nick, who fishes out the steaming brown square with tongs before pouring in another scoop of batter. It sizzles and steams.

"Wait," Willa says. "I mean—aren't those kind of competing interests? Can't Dickens just be like, *Hey you, railroad company, you should fire everyone and you'll make more money*. And then be like, *And you, federal oversight people, maybe you should fire everyone too, and then you won't have the staff to investigate all the accidents caused by firing all the railroad workers.*"

Jamie nods, just barely. "It's not quite like that," he says to

Willa, "but you're not wrong to wonder if it's ethical, advising them both."

"Kind of like working with Big Pharma and the FDA," Nick says, and Jamie says, "Kind of like that, yes."

"Dickens does that?" Willa says.

"Pretty much," Jamie says, and Willa pantomimes her angry head exploding.

"You can't love that," she says, and Jamie says, "I don't."

"I'm sorry, Jamie," my dad says. "I probably shouldn't have brought this up."

"No, no," Jamie says. "Not at all, Grandpa. It's uncomfortable to talk about, definitely, but I kind of appreciate the transparency."

"Maybe you should tell us more about Edith's gallbladder surgery," I say, and my dad laughs, launches into a different story—about the robot bridge he's been playing online—but I'm not really listening. I'm looking at the face of my son, so precious that it feels like the actual incarnation of devotion, a Byzantine halo gold leafed behind it. Jamie didn't want Miles to die, of course. Nobody did. But his death is starting to feel less like an accident than like the answer to an unholy math problem. Jamie catches my eye and smiles, and I smile back reflexively. I'm an undammable river of mother love. I'm a torch-brandishing one-woman mob, and I will go after anyone who casts doubt upon the rightness of my child. Even if that person is me.

Chapter 25

Willa is knocking on the bathroom door. "Hey, Mama, is my towel in there?"

"Don't come in here!" I yell.

"Okay, drama queen," she says. "I wasn't planning to. Is my towel in there, though?"

"I don't think so," I say. "Just give me a minute."

"What are you doing in there? Tweezing your nipple hairs?"

"Willa," I say, and she says, "Okay, okay. I'm going. I'm doing some laundry. Do you want me to strip Jamie's bed?"

"That would be great," I say calmly. "Thank you, honey." I wait until I hear her move off, then return to the situation at hand.

I have shat into a disposable plastic bucket and I am now attempting to transfer some amount of shit to a jar, using the kind of red plastic rectangle with which you might spread orange Kraft cheese onto a Keebler Club Cracker. There are no instructions about this. "Get the sample to the lab within a half hour of producing it," the lab tech had counseled, "and try not to urinate on the feces." This is something you really just don't want to hear at all, in any context—and which, by the way, is easier said than done. But I should have asked more questions, because now I'm looking at the big bucket and the small screw-top jar. How much stool constitutes a stool sample? The idea of giving someone too much of my own shit is very, very embarrassing. The fecal equivalent of a person's eyes glazing over while you're telling them about a dream you had.

Chicken is meowing and chuffing from the hallway, because a closed bathroom door always reminds the cats that they're desperate to use the litter box. The kids were like that too, when they were little. You'd be just sliding into a fragrant tub, the dishes done, everyone put to bed, when one of them would bust in to grunt out a big stinking dump and monologue, while your bath cooled, about the fact that they'd always thought the food item was pork *chob*. "But it's actually pork chop, with a *p*!" they'd be saying, explainingly, while you said, "Hmmm," and "Interesting," and "Maybe turn on the fan?" Then suddenly they'd be flushing and wriggling out of their pajamas because they were thinking they might join you, just for a bit! "Not a full *bath* bath, and definitely no hair wash. But just so you won't be lonely." And a slippery small someone would be lugging over the plastic basket of funnels and boats and squirty ducks, dumping it into the water, everything filled with phthalates and black mold. "Can I blow out this candle?" they'd say. "I don't hate perfumey smell? But I don't love-love-*love* it. Hang on. Let's turn the lights on so we can really see what we're doing!" And I wanted a minute to myself, of course. *Me time* in the quiet of the candle's glow. I could certainly talk that talk. But I loved it too. Love-love-*loved* it. Darling little body in motion. As promised, I was not lonely.

The Big Chungus bursts in finally, and Angie's here too,

now, because testing for ulcerative colitis seems to require full feline oversight. The cats watch, alarmed, from the bath mat while I wrangle excrement into the jar and put the jar in a brown paper lunch bag. Now what, though? Now there's a plastic bucket with shit in it, and the clock is ticking. I flush what's flushable. There's a recycling code on the bucket, but this is a bridge too far. Also, I see from the sticker that this item is called a "toilet hat." I should wear it to a costume party. *Oh my god, are you a stool sample?* I double-bag the hat and march it directly to the dumpster like it's a severed head.

I'm darting back out to the car now, after washing my hands first with Dr. Bronner's peppermint soap and then with Mrs. Meyer's basil dish liquid—all the groovy suds—and our small neighbor is riding by on her scooter. She stops short in the street by our driveway, calls out, "It's my sixth birthday on November second. I'm having a dinosaur birthday party."

"Fun!" I call back.

"Pin the horn on the triceratops, velociraptor cake, dino-egg piñata." She ticks these items off boredly on her fingers. "Etcetera," she says. "I had a dinosaur birthday party for my fourth birthday too."

"Fun!" I say again. "What did you do for your fifth birthday?"

She blinks at me pityingly, says, "Um, duh. I *turned five*," and scooters off, yelling behind her, "What's your favorite bird of all the birds in the world that are crows?"

"Crows," I call after her, and she calls back, "Same!"

I have one hand on the car door, but now here's my dad

emerging from the shack. I look at my watch. I have thirteen minutes to get to the lab, which is six minutes away.

"Hey, honey," he says. "What's in the bag?"

"Shit, Dad. It's actual shit."

"Really?" he says, brightening. "Are you going to the post office with it?"

I laugh. "Like, as a prank?"

"No, no," he says. "Like, are you doing one of those mail-away cancer screenings? That's what I do now, instead of the regular kind of colonoscopy. I love to picture all the mail in a big truck, just piled up alongside one of my turds." His scatological merriment is truly contagious. "There's your letter to Santa, your L.L.Bean catalogue. And there's a box with my shit floating around in it."

"I will think of that every time I bring in the mail," I say, and he laughs. "I have to hurry this specimen off to the lab," I say, and he grabs my wrist.

"Are you okay?" He looks into my eyes, his own filled with concern and framed by the tortoiseshell glasses he's always worn.

"I'm okay, Dad," I say, not crying, because I am not going to cry here in the driveway with poop in a jar in a bag and my ninety-two-year-old father worrying. Also I don't have time.

"It's not cancer?" he says, and I say, "No, no, Dad. It's not cancer."

"Okay," he says. "I indulge myself a little—in not wanting to know. I'm sorry, Rachel. I want to know it's okay, but I don't really want to hear about your suffering."

"I'm okay, Dad," I say again. "Don't be sorry. I would feel the same way if I were you. And I'm totally not suffering."

"Mom should be here to help you," he says, and I say, "I honestly don't need help. Please don't fret."

He smiles and pats my shoulder, and shuffles toward the house. "Get Willa to toast you a bagel," I call after him, and he swishes his irritated hand through the air in the universal gesture that means, *I can toast my own bagel, for fuck's sake.*

Chapter 26

Willa is wearing a Santa hat and sitting beside me on our front step, a metal mixing bowl full of colorfully wrapped hard candy between us. "Why are we giving away Zotz?" she asks, and I say, "We got a huge box of them in the mail. Press kit. The Zotz people are hoping I'll write about them, I think."

"Small dick energy," she says. "Like, *this candy is so mid we're going to fill it with fizzing chemicals.*" She pulls a purple plastic strip of candies out of the bowl, unwraps one, and pops it in her mouth. She sucks on it thoughtfully for a while. "Okay," she says. "I take it back. This candy is a whole vibe. You can quote me. Although we'll need to patch up the hole it's burning in my esophagus."

She unwraps another one and holds it out to me. "You want?" I shake my head and she puts it in her own mouth, says, "Are you not eating sugar?"

"Trying not to," I say.

"Because rash?" she says, and I shrug, say, "Because rash, I guess."

I'm wondering about sarcoidosis, the granulomatous disease doctor has written in the portal. *Could explain rash, blood work, liver findings. Lungs clear on CT. Referring to a retinologist.* Sarcoidosis can affect your eyes, apparently. At least if I lose my vision I won't have to look at the rash anymore!

Every morning I wake up to inspect it—the plaques and macules and papules and pustules behind my knees and all over my thighs, shins, calves, ankles, arms, chest, and shoulders—and every morning Nick says, "Looking a little better, right?" "I don't think so, no," I say, and he makes a sad face. "What's the plan here, folks?" I say—I'm talking to my immune system, but nobody ever answers. How stupid is this—having a body that's a hypochondriac? It's just creating imaginary problems and attacking its own skin and organs and scaring itself half to death. Sometimes I sit quietly with the meditation app Audio-Mune™. *I am well*, I think. *I am whole. Fuck.*

It's gorgeous out—a little bewilderingly mild, but so burnished and pretty. We've moved on from the Crayola candy-corn oranges and yellows of the maple trees to the adult colors of the oaks: bourbon and cognac and red wine. I am still not drinking.

"I love the oak trees," I sigh, and Willa says, "Of course you do. You also love the boring brown female cardinals instead of the pretty red males. You are very attuned to subtlety."

"Are you teasing me?" I say, and she says, "I am."

The light is fading, and the trick-or-treaters are emerging from the darkness—hordes of Marvel characters and video-game characters and movie spin-off characters, none of which I have any referent for. There are occasional throwbacks too—witches and ghosts and Alf—and some very homemade costumes that are, like, cotton balls hot-glued onto a gray sweatshirt or a cardboard box spray-painted to look like something or other, and I don't know what they are or mean. I especially love the defiant and abashed teenagers in their fishnet stockings and black lipstick: the sexy nurses and sexy cats and sexy—whatever this is. The Pope? The wholesomeness of filling a pillowcase with candy, when they could just be snorting lines of cocaine out of each other's butt cracks, makes me want to cry.

Halloween is when you can really get to know your kids and their secret selves. The year Willa was two, she wrapped a silky green scarf around herself and when anyone asked what she was, she said, annoyed, "Green scarf." ("Geen scoff!" Nick and I still growl bitterly to each other.) The next year, she made me make her a snake costume, even though she was desperately afraid of them. Then she was a robber, a pirate, a vampire, Voldemort. We were worried we were going to have to draw the line at, like, Pol Pot. Bernie Madoff. But then she veered from evil back to benign weirdness: she was a Yankee candle, a parking ticket, a xylophone, lettuce. Even just last year I found myself with a mouthful of pins, running a human-sized butternut squash through my sewing machine. "How is this still happening?" I complained, and Willa, presiding bossily over the costume-making, sighed like an innocent and said, "I wish I knew."

She greets all of our little neighbors by name, exclaims over their capes and masks, encourages them to take bigger handfuls of candy. I seem to be in charge only of munching on the pumpkin seeds I've roasted with butter and Old Bay seasoning. The smell of singed squash guts is wafting out of our illuminated jack-o'-lantern, but I'm too lazy to deal with it. We call out, "Happy Halloween!" and "Oh my god, look at you guys!" and, after the little kids are prompted to thank us by their parents, "You're so welcome!"

"Did you see it was Miles Zapf's birthday?" Willa asks me during a lull, and I say I did. "Facebook is so weird," she says. "The way there are a bunch of people still wishing him well."

"I know," I say. "I saw that too." It had been a mix of broken-heart emojis and "Have a great day! Let's catch up soon." His mother had posted a picture of him—pinkly newborn and swaddled in a hospital blanket—and said she was missing her baby. My heart turned into a closed fist, and I had to mentally pry its fingers open so I could hold her grief.

"He seems like he was kind of a weird person," I hear myself say to Willa now, and cringe.

She turns to look at me. "I mean, sure. Yeah. So am I. What do you mean?"

"I don't know." I shake my head. "Just that—I don't know. That dance community—most of them seem so much older than him. It's not super hard to imagine that he was lonely. Or kind of isolated. So many of his friends don't even seem to know he died."

Willa sighs, presses her lips together before saying, "Mom, don't."

"Don't what?" I say.

"Don't make a case for his suicide so you can imagine that Jamie's blameless." She reaches her hand into the bowl of seeds and I turn my head away. We're quiet while she chews, the moon rising up big and orange behind the house across the street from ours. "I'm sorry, Mama," she says.

"Don't be," I say. I'm trying not to cry. "I think you might be right."

A group of kids is approaching, so I wipe my eyes on the cuff of my sweatshirt to properly admire the five superheroes and one slot machine. Some of the parents say, "Trick or treat," and hold out empty or half-empty wineglasses, and I fill them from the big bottle of red I've got beside me on the step because it's a neighborhood tradition. The kids stuff their bags and buckets with Zotz, and Willa points out a plastic orange jack-o'-lantern pail and surreptitiously pantomimes vomiting into it.

She turns back to me after they recede into the darkness. "It's not, like, a nature show, Mama," she says. I don't know what she means. "The way one episode is focused on the gazelles so you hope the lions don't kill and eat them, but then a different episode is focused on the lions, so you hope they do." I understand. "You can't just lean into the suicide angle all of a sudden because you're rooting for another team now. I mean, you can? But I don't think it's right."

"So, what's right?" I say.

"What do you mean?" she says. "Like, what's the right way to process the Jamie piece?"

"I guess," I say. "Yeah."

"I don't know," she says, and is quiet for moment. "I guess I'm thinking about Jamie's net positive impact in the world. Like, the way he's so fun and nice and helps everyone and makes their lives better and brighter. How he plays Frank Sinatra on the piano for Grandpa and always checks on me, sends me funny videos when he knows I'm sad. Or when I was visiting him and Maya in the city last month—Jamie knew everyone on the street."

I shake my head. I don't know what this means.

"From the soup kitchen where he volunteers. Like, he knows *everyone*. You should go down and walk around his neighborhood with him. Every gritty person you pass is like, 'Jaaamiiieee!' And he's so cute and clean-cut. He's all sweet and shy, like, 'Oh, hi! So nice to see you!' It's the best."

"I don't think I realized he was still doing that." This was an initiative at his last job—where everyone was supposed to do a volunteer shift at an organization of their choosing. I'd thought maybe the soup kitchen was a one-off.

"He goes every weekend," she says.

"That's so good," I say, and she says, "I know."

It's late, but here's a final straggler: a gorgeous teenager done up with ripped tights and swoops of black hair and black eyeliner, carrying her loot around in what looks like just a nice leather tote bag.

"Cutie!" I whisper, and Willa says, "Mom. Don't."

"I love your sexy-goth costume," I say, and she smiles at me, extends her hand. I hold the bowl of candy out to her, and Willa says, "Oh my god, Mom. Stop."

"Hey," the girl says, and Willa reaches out to take her hand and rises up from the step.

"Oh!" I say.

"Mom, this is Ruby. Ruby, my mom, who thinks you're a trick-or-treater."

When she laughs, I get to see all of Ruby's pretty teeth. "Oh god," I say. "I'm so sorry. I forgot you said you were going out tonight. Nice to meet you, Ruby."

"Nice to meet you too," Ruby says to me, although she's smiling at my daughter. And I offer them a mug of hot cider, a bowl of black bean soup, a ride into town, but they don't want anything, they're just going to walk—and there they go, down the road, illuminated by the streetlights and the moon and by some other kind of radiance, although I know I'm a romantic. I know.

It's just me on the step now with a burning pumpkin and an empty bowl of its seeds. I have so much to think about that my mind has gone suspiciously blank. But that's okay, because the door opens and Nick, who's been in the basement gluing or sawing or sanding something, comes out and sits down beside me.

"How was it?" he says.

"It was good," I say. "It was a lot."

"The trick-or-treaters were a lot?" he asks, and I say, "I don't know. Yeah."

"Did my dad go to bed?" I say, and Nick says, "I think he's watching *Vera*. Listen."

British crime drama is indeed emanating from the shack. "Are you telling me how to do my job?" Vera scolds someone in her Northumberland accent, and I hear my father's delighted laughter.

I lean against Nick, and he wraps an arm around my waist. From the woods at the end of our street, an owl hoots, and I shudder.

"Are you okay?" Nick says, and I say, "I honestly have no idea."

Chapter 27

It's our second voyage into Boston this week. Happily, the retinologist has divined nothing alarming inside my eyeballs—no evidence of granulomatous activity or scarring, although my vision is as terrible as ever—and next up is the MRI of my liver. It's only a two-hour trip, although it feels long today. Some of the trees along the highway still have a scrim of beige leaves on them, but mostly they're bare. The sky is white. Because this MRI is the type of test you need to fast for, I'm hungry and uncaffeinated, and I warn Nick about this.

"I'm in kind of a dangerous November mood," I say, and he says, "Noted."

"I mean: Thank you for driving me," I say, and he laughs and turns some music on so he'll have a better shot at us not interacting.

I check my email, where there's a message from the spatchcocking editor that they've held the piece so long that now they're going to publish it as part of their Thanksgiving package, and I'll need to adapt all the recipes. *Can you just run your eyes over the attached? Make sure it's all fine for turkey (18 to 24 lbs) instead of chicken. Need to adjust cooking time and temp, brining. Cut grilling. Add gravy sidebar—giblets, etc.* I turn green, bulge up with enormous muscles, burst out of my clothes, and Incredible Hulk my way to the editor's New York office, where I snap him in half like a wishbone. *You blithering thundercunt*, I type and delete. *I literally still don't even have a contract for this piece*, I type and delete. *This edit feels beyond the scope of the original assignment*, I type. I don't delete it, but I don't hit SEND either. How badly do I want to write for him again? I do the money math, accounting for the fact that I've recently been fired from my own motherfucking etiquette column. So: pretty badly, I guess. I delete what I've written. *Sure*, I write. *Give me to the end of the week to do a little testing and tinkering.* I hit SEND and breathe deeply and steadily while I listen to Nina Simone sing about how good she's feeling. It's a new dawn, it's a new day. "Prepare to eat turkey all week," I say glumly, and Nick says, "Great! I love turkey!" "Please etch *giblets, etcetera* onto my tombstone," I say, and he says, "Will do."

Nick drops me off so he can park and then go for a run while I do my scan. I lean into the open driver's-side window to kiss him good-bye. "Good luck," he says, because what else can you say? In the waiting room, I am given a contrast solution to sip slowly over the next half hour. An old man in a wheelchair lifts his own bottle toward me and says, "Cheers, baby."

"Cheers," I say back, and I walk over to clink my bottle against his.

"Better than the CAT scan," he says.

"The one that makes you feel like you wet yourself?" I say.

"Yes, that one," he says, and laughs. It's the most uncanny experience of sudden, spreading warmth. "Oops!" I said out loud after they started the IV, and the tech said, "No, no. You're good. You're not actually peeing. It just feels like that."

"Let's hope for good results for both of us," my old comrade says to me comfortingly, and I hold up my crossed fingers. I am the youngest patient here by twenty years, but these are my people nonetheless.

When they call me back, he says to the tech, "Take good care of my girl here," and I blow him a kiss.

The intake person asks a trillion questions to make sure I don't have secret metal in my body that will shoot up into my brain and kill me as soon as the magnet's on. "Fillings," I say, and open my mouth to show her my many prodigiously repaired teeth. She shakes her head and laughs. "Those are okay," she says. She runs through her list: "Artificial limbs or joints? Pacemaker? Defibrillator? Insulin pump? Shrapnel? Have you swallowed a GI camera pill in the last week?" "Gosh, I don't think so?" I say. Suddenly I'm less sure than I should be. Also: People have a lot going on, it turns out! Shrapnel. Jesus. "Do you have an older IUD?" she asks, and I think, *Do I? God, did I ever get my IUD removed?* A relic from a different time, like the expired ketchup at the back of the fridge from when the kids were eight. "Oh," I say, remembering. "I think it fell out on its own at some point." She laughs, says it wouldn't likely be a problem anyway and she's going to check *no*. "Could you be pregnant?" is her final question, and I say, sadly, that I could not be. "At least I don't think I could," I add, because all certainty has evaporated, despite the fact that any ova I still have must be fossils by now. I picture the hundred-year-old egg Willa tasted in a Malaysian restaurant, the white tinted an unsettlingly translucent shade of green.

I change into the skidless socks and a cloth johnny, put my own clothes in a middle school locker, and try to avoid the bin with a SOILED LINENS sign that makes me feel like everyone shat themselves even though I know it just means *used*. When I pop out, the tech escorts me past the illuminated red sign warning that the MAGNET IS ALWAYS ON into a freezing room where there's a loud, steady whooshing like a fetal heartbeat. After I lie down on the table, she drapes me with a blanket from the warmer, and I groan.

"This is so good," I say. "I'm just going to take a little nap."

"No, no," she laughs. "We need you awake! You have to hold your breath for part of the test." I had forgotten. She puts headphones on me and presses a rubbery gray bulb into my palm, which I can squeeze to alert them if I'm losing it inside the tube. The camera sits on my chest and stomach, and it's nice and heavy, like a dog's ThunderShirt. The ceiling above me is made up of the same cardboardy white tiles as every other one of the many medical ceilings I've looked up at over the past few months, complete with the requisite leaking-corpse stains.

The tech slides me into the tube, asks through the headphones how I am. I'm good. She tells me that she's going to start the scan and that she'll let me know when to hold my breath. Inside the machine, it sounds like a German disco in the 1980s. The rhythmic whooshing is punctuated by other, louder sounds: a fire alarm, a dog whistle, an electric drill, something banging. "Hold your breath," the tech says suddenly into the headphones, and I'm caught off guard, haven't taken a big enough breath to prepare, feel like I'm suffocating. "Okay, breathe," she says, and then, a second later, "Hold." I can't get the rhythm right. Then again, I've never even been able to swim the crawl without feeling like I'm drowning. I try not to hyperventilate from either performance anxiety or claustrophobia. It's so dark in here! But then I realize that I've got my eyes squeezed shut, and when I open them it's perfectly light and normal and I can just breathe in a regular way.

One thing has led to another, is what I'm thinking. One minute, you're with all the healthy people on the beach, everyone enjoying the sunshine and salt spray, maybe tossing a Frisbee around. And then suddenly you're alone in the waves, getting yanked out to sea by some kind of medical undertow, the shore receding from view while all the healthy people wave to you pityingly.

Every Sunday I fill two different day-of-the-week pill organizers. One contains the single big dose of methotrexate, which is twelve pills, along with the daily megadose of folic acid to counteract the methotrexate's side effects, plus the daily Zoloft (so I won't be such a screwball) and daily vitamin D3 and a new twice-daily immunosuppressant called Rebuqtanofib. Or Rebukofide? Or maybe some other completely dreadful and seemingly random combination of syllables. It's one of those drugs you see ads for at odd hours when you're watching television because you can't sleep on account of your autoimmune disease. "I'll soon be running deliriously through fields of wildflowers," I said, when my doctor told me she was calling it in. "Or so I have been led to imagine." The commercial ends on a cheerful montage of invisibly ill people selecting aged cheeses and cured meats from a charcuterie board while the narrator speed-talks through the panoply of side effects: dry cuticles and scratchy throat and nosebleeds; lymphoma and stroke and sudden death. "But should I take Rebukofide if I'm *allergic* to Rebukofide?" I always ask Nick, right before the commercial tells you that no, you shouldn't. On the TV, our weirdly ecstatic patient fingers another slice of prosciutto. "What if I'm just allergic to the *ingredients* in Rebukofide?" I ask—but no, the voice says, not then either.

The other pill organizer? This is my secret black-magic pill organizer that I fill beneath a cloak of shame, when nobody else is home. It's a mix of actual substances and invented ones: massive tablets of quercetin (?) and LiverFriend; hard, plasticky capsules of turmeric and bovine colostrum that I stole from a calf; and some big, rubbery ones too—fish oil and glutathione (?) and vitamin E. You have to assume that at some point I'll turn into a different animal altogether, and it's all very humiliating, although I did run the list by "my pharmacist" (the teenager who works at CVS) to make sure there were no drug interaction issues. I also keep a tub of probiotic capsules in the fridge, and this is my alibi. When the doctors ask me what else I'm taking besides the prescriptions I've got on file, I cop only to the acidophilus, the lactobacillus. "Nothing else?" they ask suspiciously, because I'm wearing clogs and smell like lentil burgers. "No other supplements?" *Oh, just the hocus-pocus ones!* I don't say, because I know it will sound like alchemy—like I'm burning lead and sulfur under a full moon and imploring the goddesses to turn it all into gold or good health. "No other supplements," I say. When Jamie was a baby, and the pediatrician would ask if he was sleeping through the night, I said, "Yup!" because if I told them that he woke in our bed to nurse every thirty-five seconds, I was going to get a big lecture. And I didn't want to get a big lecture. Each magic pill is approximately four inches long, and the potential irony—that I will choke to death on a health supplement—is not lost on me.

"You're all set," the tech is saying to me through the headphones now. "I'm going to come and get you." I am retrieved from the tunnel, reunited with my clothing and phone, and ejected out onto the sunny sidewalk, where I text Nick that I'm done. My waiting-room companion is sitting in his wheelchair by the curb.

He smiles semi-toothfully, says, "How was it?"

"Okay," I say, and shrug. "You?"

"Long," he says, and laughs. "I didn't think it would still be light out."

"I know," I say. "It's like coming out of a matinee. I guess time didn't stop for anybody else."

"It's like that old soap opera," he says, and I say, "*General Hospital?*"

"No," he says.

"*Days of Our Lives?*" I say. "Like sands through the hourglass?"

"No," he says.

"I'm out of soap operas," I say, but he remembers, says, "*As the World Turns.*"

"Oh!" I say. "Yes. The world just, kind of, keeps on turning. While you're getting irradiated in a weird tunnel."

"Exactly," he says.

"Can we give you a ride somewhere?" I ask. "My husband is coming in a car."

"Nah," he says. "But thank you. My wife is coming too. How lucky are we?"

"So lucky," I say. "Plus I get to appreciate that I don't have any shrapnel in my body."

"I do," he says, and laughs. "But it's just in my leg—the one I've still got—so it was fine."

"Oh god!" I say. "I'm so sorry." Sorry you were in a war. Sorry you were injured. Sorry I'm such an asshole. I try to do the math in my head. Korea? I picture him with all his teeth and legs, unfolding a love letter from his wife before being blown not quite to smithereens.

"No," he says. "Don't be. You have to appreciate anything you can appreciate. I'm happy to be alive. That's you?" Nick is waving to me from the Subaru.

"That's me," I say. "Can I wait with you?"

My shrapnel-filled friend shakes his head, holds out his fist. When I bump it, he says, "Go get it, lucky girl," and I tell him I will.

Chapter 28

It starts innocently enough: waking, tossing, turning, fretting, stewing, vowing not to get my phone, and then tiptoeing downstairs in the dark to get my phone. But I'm only going to look at fun stuff! Silly stuff. And it's like that at first—it is.

I watch a recipe video of a home cook making something called "Brazilian Lemonade" that looks to be whole lemons blended with ice and sweetened condensed milk, and it's all I can do not to run downstairs and make some. I don't really expect commenters to share my enthusiasm, but still the vitriol is kind of shocking. *Literal garbage*, someone has written. *A great recipe if you want to spend the rest of your life on the toilet or mainlining insulin*, someone else has, while doubtless swigging from a sixty-four-ounce frosted eggnog mochaccino with an extra shot of corn syrup. Because there is no online offering too inconsequential to occasion racist vitriol, there is also this: *Don't they have gloves in Brazil? What is wrong with these people?* This commenter must be the kind of sanitation expert who puts on gloves before using his own blender, toothbrush, or swastika template. *Your gloved finger could have been jammed into someone's bare asshole*, I write and delete. *That recipe looks delicious*, I write instead, before opening our bedroom window and having the rest of my hot flash.

On Buy Nothing, someone is offering to gift a tarp with many holes in it, which feels so excessively pointless—like a raincoat that's no longer waterproof, which, in fact, is what someone else is offering. *Might make a nice pet bed*, the raincoat person has mused. Really? A crumbly old Gore-Tex jacket with frayed Velcro at the cuffs? Might it? Actually, the cats would probably love crinkling around on it, but still. Someone wants to *gift* a pair of rotisserie chicken carcasses, which have been stored in the freezer and which have been photographed inside of a large Ziploc bag that is entirely frosted over. You just have to, kind of, imagine they're in there, waiting to be made into freezer-burn soup stock. Someone has offered a dozen tuna sandwiches that didn't get eaten at a scout meeting, although there is no mention of the bonus case of salmonella you're surely being gifted. Someone is giving away a collection of pet supplements, including half a tub of JurrasiCal reptile calcium, which doesn't agree with her poor, frail-boned gecko. Someone else is giving away a collection of human supplements, partially used, some of which are the very same supplements I myself take. *No longer needed*, they've written, ambiguously. *Because the person taking them got better or because they died?* I want to ask. ("For sale: baby shoes, never worn.") Oh, but here's something nice! A pair of cut-crystal candlesticks. Ha ha, they're Jo's! Probably a gift from her rich aunt who shops only at Tiffany & Co. *These are perfectly lovely*, she's written. *Just not our style.* I write what I always write when Jo offers anything here: *I can't believe you're giving away the wedding present we gave you!* with a crying-face emoji.

I turn my phone all the way off, lie in the dark with my

eyes open, then turn my phone back on and wait for it to light up. I look at the children's Instagram accounts to see if they've been tagged in any recent pictures, and they have. Willa is with Ruby and Sunny in a wholesome selfie that seems to have been taken on my bed and showcases Chicken and Angie asleep on their backs, tummies up. Jamie is in a series of chaotic bar photos, where his tie seems to get looser and looser as the night progresses. His boyish beauty, usually a source of swelling pleasure, gives me a constricted feeling, like guilt. Regret. Who posted these photos? Some guy with the Roman numeral *III* after his name. I click on his profile and scroll around. Expensive-looking sweaters, nice watch, lots of brown liquor. Probably he works for Dickens. I am very, very careful, as the kids have schooled me to be, not to like anything or leave a trace. Oops! No, I'm not. I have liked his current story, which shows him playing a ball sport in Central Park. Rugby? Does rugby have balls? Polo? Fuck. Worse comes to worst, what could happen? The guy shows it to Jamie, says, *Dude, the person who liked my story—is this your* mom? *What's she doing, Jamie—trying to figure out who you even are?*

I turn my phone all the way off, scooch over to wrap my arm around Nick's warm back, then scooch back to grab my phone and turn it back on. My patient portal is still open in a browser window, but it wants me to log back in, and I do. Here, under the test results tab, is the MRI Cholangiopancreatography (MRCP) with Contrast, which I have already looked at. But I look again. The good news is that there are many, many things I hadn't known to worry about—and that I don't have! No lymphadenopathy. No abdominal aortic aneurysm.

No renal hydronephrosis. No masses or fluid in either my peritoneum or my retroperitoneum, which are bonus body parts I didn't even know I had! No nodules in my adrenal glands. No masses in my pancreas. No effusions in my lower chest. No focal lesions in my spleen. Somewhat surprisingly, there is no evidence of granulomatous disease anywhere in my abdomen, which speaks against the sarcoidosis diagnosis. I do have a hemangioma in my T11 vertebral body, but when I google this, it seems to be a kind of benign tumor of the spine that is largely untroubling. I also have various cysts of various dimensions in my liver and kidneys—also unconcerning, allegedly, although I'm not overjoyed to read about them. *Why are you making all these pointless growths?* I silently ask my organs, and they respond by chuckling and making more of them.

Here's the thing, though. It's only one thing, really. A single sentence. This single sentence: *Beaded appearance of intrahepatic biliary ductal system in bilateral lobes, may represent primary sclerosing cholangitis.* The "Radiologist Diagnostic Certainty Scale" is included to help me interpret the word *may*.

Most likely means very high probability
Likely means high probability
May represent means intermediate probability
Unlikely means low probability
Very unlikely means very low probability

There is an intermediate probability that I have a bile-duct disease called primary sclerosing cholangitis, which, according to every single article I've now read online, is untreatable and ends in liver transplant or liver failure and death. The median survival time without transplant is ten years, which means I have a decade left to make videos for the kids about—what? What would I hope to tell their future selves? Console the grieving, love big, write your elected officials, send thank-you notes, never worry about filling up on the passed hors d'oeuvres. I believe I have already imparted these vital nuggets. I'd make better use of my remaining time on Earth by sucking up to people who look like they have healthy livers. *Oooh, that mocktail looks delicious! I'm Rocky. Hey, what are you doing next Friday?*

Despite the fact that primary sclerosing cholangitis is strongly correlated with ulcerative colitis, that test has come back negative. I have googled around for other possible causes of a "beaded appearance of the intrahepatic biliary ductal system," but there really don't seem to be any. Just this one frightening disease that will progress unchecked and end badly. How do so many people live to be old? It seems utterly improbable and impossibly lucky. I've already left a fretful message for the granulomatous disease doctor, asking her to refer me ASAP to a liver person. Now I shine the light from my phone screen over my legs, which look mottled and purple tonight. *Purpuric* is the medical term. I half expect the rash to arrange itself into the letters *SOS*. Did my liver do all this? Also, how awkward is it going to be to tell people? *Yeah, it's bad. Primary sclerosing cholangitis. No, no—you've never heard of it. Yeah, in the liver. No, no it's not from drinking that Fireball nip I found in the pocket of the coat I got from the Goodwill. At least I hope not, ha ha!* Would it kill me to get just a regular terminal disease like everybody else?

Hoping to amplify the whispers of good news, I google the

word *retroperitoneum* and find this definition: "the anatomical space (sometimes a potential space) behind the peritoneum. It has no specific delineating anatomical structures." So, in the space that's maybe only a potential space and also has nothing in it, at least there are no masses or fluid! It feels like the kind of diagnostic silver lining that should be accompanied by a surrealist painting of a black hole. *I'm going to die* is what I'm thinking, fear banging away like a drum in my brain—unless that's just my actual heart beating.

I click over to Reddit to see if anyone's talking about primary sclerosing cholangitis, but am distracted by new content on the subreddit r/railroaders, which I've been stalking. The subject of the new post is "Railroader Mother Seeking Advice." *Please help*, the poster has written before going on to describe a fatal accident in Florida that her conductor son was involved in. *He's been driving that train for only two years*, she writes. *It seems like maybe a suicide, a car on the tracks, god rest. First they said drugs but now they say my son may have had a "sleep incident." What can I do to support him? He's shaken up and worried they're going to remove him from service due to mental health.* The post has generated a wide range of responses, from folks commiserating or telling her just to be a shoulder to cry on, to outrage about the likelihood of broken signaling equipment. There is some cruelty too. *LMFAO*, someone has written. *Sleep incident means your dude was dozing. Wake the fuck up, you're driving the train.*

I read every single response. Someone has asked the OP (original poster) for clarification about whether the implied drug user was her son or the driver of the car, and she's responded that it was her son. Someone else has thought to mention that the train itself would have been unscathed by this encounter: *Maybe a mark on the knuckle, but that would be all*, which occasions a long digression about the relative solidity of trains; a train hitting a car is like a car hitting a soda can, many different people point out. Someone has recommended that the son forgo any mental health care offered directly by the railroad, where confidentiality seems to be an issue. This warning prompts someone else to lament the fact that the railroad has enlisted a company called Workforce 24/7 to train everyone to stay awake during dangerously long shifts. *Yeah*, another commenter writes in response, *that's instead of hiring the right number of people for coverage. It's all management consulting advice.* Don't worry, we understand the dangers of fatigue! We talked to the sleep people!

Don't they assign a dollar amount to a lost life? someone asks in this same thread, and yes, they do—this is called the VSL, the value of a statistical life, and it seems to run around five million dollars in the bleak arithmetic of risk assessment.

And then, jarringly, there's a photograph of the accident. *This your boy's train?* someone has written. *Bro*, someone else has written. *Take that down. These people are suffering.* These mothers. The mother of the wracked train conductor. Miles's mother, looking—or not looking—at a photo just like this. Me, maybe, although my son is a victim only of the industry he waded into willingly, blindly, with dollar signs for eyes.

The train that hit Miles's car? The freight it was carrying included snow melt—the salt you spread on icy roads to keep the drivers safe.

"Cheer up—it might never happen!" my own mum said,

Britishly, if you were glum. But then, sometimes, it did happen. It does. Sometimes it's an accident: a single moment slicing your world in half to create a before and an after. Not inevitable, but it happens nonetheless. Like the time Jamie flipped out of a hammock and smashed out his two front teeth on our concrete patio. A minute earlier, I'd have been out there still; a minute later, I'd have already called him inside for dinner. I cuddled and consoled and mopped up blood and filled a bag with ice and then, when Nick got home, knelt on the bathroom floor with my forehead pressed to the cold tiles until I could stand again. The teeth were only baby teeth—but the blood was actual blood. "I can't wait to see what the tooth fairy brings for *this*!" Jamie lisped, because he was a silver linings kind of kid. He still is. And I still have a rattly little box of the kids' molars and bicuspids in my jewelry box, like a talisman.

We have fallen back so the sun is rising early, and I turn my phone off, drag the snoring cats up to my neck, and try to close my eyes. The tooth fairy brought three Sacagawea dollar coins, I'm remembering. One for each tooth and one for the accident. Sacagawea was a mother too. I don't turn my phone back on to learn what happened to her children—but I fall asleep thinking about them.

Chapter 29

Willa is suddenly standing by my bed in tears. I'm reading, and Nick is in the shack helping my dad with his BritBox. She has googled *methotrexate* and discovered that it's a kind of chemotherapy. "I'm worried you have cancer and aren't telling me," she says, and I say, "I don't, honey. I really, truly don't." She climbs into bed, and I remember a scared Willa from years ago—she'd awoken from a nightmare she couldn't tell us. I placed a flat palm on her bony chest and felt the way her heart galloped like a wild horse. So afraid and alive. Now I turn on my side to face her, and I push her hair out of her damp face. "I don't like being lied to," she says, like a warning. I almost joke, "Oh, that's weird, most people *love* being lied to," but I realize in the nick of time that it's not funny—and that some people, like her own grandfather, actually do like being lied to. Instead I say, "I know you don't, honey," and hope I'm not lying to her.

What's true is that the rash is spreading like mold, all the splotches merging together now like biscuits rising in a pan. There's a scene in *The Cat in the Hat Comes Back* where the pink cat ring—the one that has been migrating around the house from tub to shoes to rug—gets flung outside and turns the snow a mottled salmon color. The more the kids work at eliminating it, the pinker it gets, until the cat unleashes something called Voom from his hat, and all of it disappears. I'm waiting for my Voom, I guess. Although last night we did see a commercial for a different immunosuppressant drug from the one I'm taking—everybody wincing in pain, clawing at their arms, and then suddenly playing water polo and backgammon, euphorically eating cotton candy—and Willa said, "Mom! Ask your doctor if Sovlenka Lexphoria is right for you." "I was seriously just thinking that," I said, and I was.

"Um, Mama," Willa is saying. "When I came in? Were you cutting your hair with nail clippers?"

"No."

"I mean, you were."

"I was just trimming the front a little."

"With nail clippers."

"The scissors are in that basket." I point across the room. "The nail clippers were right here."

"Mom," she says.

"I know," I say. "I was just freshening up the layers."

"Are you going out?"

"I was supposed to," I say. "But Jo has something. A painful cyst? Where her legs meet."

Willa blinks at me. "Her vag?"

"No, no," I say. "I'm sure it's not her vag. Maybe her groin?"

"That's not where your legs meet," she says. "That's where one leg meets your body. Her *taint*?"

"Hang on," I say. "I'm texting her. Oh yeah, you're right," I say, and show Willa Jo's text, which says, *Taint my groin, alas.*

Willa laughs, shakes her head, and says, "Why are *slot* and *slit* two different words? And they're both embarrassing."

"I don't know," I say.

"Is it mail slot or mail slit? Oh, it's *slot*. I can hear it. It's not a slit machine either. Why do we even need *slit*?"

"I don't know," I say.

We lie quietly for a minute before Willa says, "Someone at the lab has an emotional support pigeon named Cheese that she wears in a clear backpack."

"That's weird," I say, and Willa says, "I know! But I wish I could bring Angie everywhere." At the sound of her name, Angie leaps up onto Willa's hip and begins frantically washing her white socks and mittens. "Excuse me," Willa scolds. "I'm not just a bathing platform for cats. Oh, now you're washing your little kitten bumhole? That's silly."

"Oh, hey, you got a reminder postcard from Dr. Vagina about scheduling your annual," I remember suddenly.

"Ugh," she says. "Okay."

"Remember when you thought it was pap *schmear*," I say, "like cream cheese on a bagel?"

"I still sometimes say, 'Just a light schmear,' when she cranks open the speculum."

I laugh. "Am I going to get to meet Ruby again?" I say, and she says, "Ew, Mom. Did gynecology remind you?"

"Oh god, I don't think so," I say. "I don't know what made me think of that."

"Yes," she says, poker-faced. "I think it's very likely that you will meet Ruby again."

"Oooh. Is it good?" I say, and she says, grinning now, "I think it's good."

"How did you actually meet?"

"We met at Cracker Barrel."

"Really?"

"Yes! We bumped right into each other at the . . . barrel? Getting our crackers? No. Mom. We met on Tinder. That's how people meet."

"Oh," I say. "Yes."

"That's how I met Jack too. But yikes. She sure Jekyll-and-Hyded me half to death."

"The worst!" I say. This was Willa's college girlfriend who brought a year of tiny little midriff-baring sweaters and Dentyne cinnamon chewing gum and nerve-racking drama into our lives. "But—sorry—what was the Jekyll part?"

"Yeah, that's probably the wrong reference. Just different versions of being controlling and kind of a dick. I guess Hyde and Hyde." She pauses, touches a single fingertip to the biggest mole on my face for no reason. I swat her hand away. "Remember when Jamie and I were confused about Take a Penny, Leave a Penny?"

"Oh my god," I say. I had forgotten—the way I would watch them at the old candy store in town, carefully removing a penny from the little saucer near the cash register and then carefully putting it back. They did this for years—it turned out they thought the sign was an imperative. "You guys were very literal."

"We really were. Remember when we were so scared in San Francisco because you said that place was a tourist trap?" I do.

I couldn't figure out why they didn't want to get bread bowls full of soup at Fisherman's Wharf, but it turned out they were expecting a big cage to drop down on them like in a cartoon. Meanwhile, I'd seen a road sign that said EMERGENCY EVACUATION ROUTE and vibrated with fear the whole time, waiting for a tsunami to wash us out to sea with our clam chowder.

Willa sighs now. "I want to be there for Jamie," she says, and I say, "Of course you do, honey. I'm sure he knows that."

"Yeah, but it seems like he doesn't really need anything. I feel like I'm just, kind of, holding sadness about Miles. Like, on Jamie's behalf."

"That sounds helpful," I say uncertainly. I'm not totally sure what she means.

"Do you understand what I mean?" she says, and I say, "I'm not totally sure."

"Me either," she says. "I guess I'm just being supportive in kind of a vibes way."

"I am confident he feels very loved by you," I say truthfully.

"But do you think he feels like I'm judging him?" she says. This is a good question.

"I don't know. Are you judging him?"

"I don't know." She shakes her head, sits up with her phone.

"Who are you texting?"

"Dad. I heard him come in. I'm asking him to make us some Corn Chex nachos." When I look at her over the top of my reading glasses, she says, "I'm a baby and a big girl," which is something she used to say about herself when she was little and wanted to be carried but without ceding any of her dignity.

"What'd he say?"

She lies down again. "He said, 'Make your own Corn Chex nachos.'"

"Seriously?"

"Of course not! He said he'll bring them right up. Mom, are you going to be healthy?"

"Oh," I say. "Yeah. That's my plan. Grandpa got me a gift subscription to the Mayo Clinic newsletter for my birthday. I read it cover to cover this morning, so at least there's that."

We hear the microwave beep, hear Nick on the stairs singing, "Egrets, I've seen a few, but then again . . ." and here he is with a plateful of cereal covered in molten cheddar and Frank's Red Hot.

"Your nachos," he says, with a flourish, then squeezes onto the bed next to Willa. We pull off stretchy clumps, chew them contentedly.

"Worldwide, how many households a day do you think make nachos out of Corn Chex?" Willa says, and Nick says, quickly, "Twenty-five thousand." Willa and I look at each other and laugh. "What?" he says. "How many do you think?"

"I was literally going to say one," Willa says.

"I was thinking three to five," I say.

"Wow," Nick says. "What did I say? Two hundred and fifty thousand? That may have been an overestimate."

I laugh. "I think you just said twenty-five thousand."

"Even that," he says, and shakes his head. "I guess I find it hard to believe that people are so different from me. It's such a missed opportunity."

"Corn Chex nachos?" Willa says. "Or being like you?"

"I guess both," Nick says.

Now we're scraping up the waxy ends of the cheddar with our thumbnails. Willa feeds a tiny piece to Angie, scolding her the whole time for being so small and eating cheese.

"Is my dad okay?" I say, and Nick says, "He's good. He wanted me to remind you to make a double batch of stuffing this year. And to make sure the cranberry sauce is sweet enough."

"I'm sure he'll be coming in to oversee the holiday preparations," I say, and Willa laughs. We have many photographs of me whisking the gravy or draining the green beans or carving the turkey while my dad stands by monitoringly, bent slightly forward at the waist with his hands behind his back. *Oh, Jews do that too?* a friend commented on my Instagram photo once. *I thought it was only Korean grandfathers.*

"Is everybody coming?" Willa says, and I say, "Everybody's coming." This is our usual Thanksgiving crowd: The four of us plus Maya and my dad. Jo's family. Nick's two cousins from Boston. And then a few stragglers—a couple of neighbors, three of Willa's international lab-mates, and an old college friend of Jamie's who lives in the area.

"Are you making me the good kind of tofu?"

"I am."

"Are you making me vegetarian gravy?"

"Yes."

"And at least one pie that's not pecan?"

"Yes."

"Can it be the cranberry-cheesecake one?"

"Sure."

"Okay," Nick says uneasily. "But I still think it makes sense to make two pecan pies because it's so many people."

"I got you, honey," I say.

"More carrots, less radishes, in terms of veggies for dipping," Willa says.

"Noted."

"Did you get hit by a tranquilizer dart?" Willa says. "You're so un-irritated by us."

"Actually," I say. "I felt like I was getting a migraine and Grandpa gave me half a Valium."

"Oh my god, Mom."

"I know," I say. I reach over to twist off my bedside light. Willa and Nick laugh in the sudden dark.

"Um, good night," Nick says, and I fall asleep before they're even done mocking me.

Chapter 30

The kitchen door opens, and here's my dad, shaking off the rain, wishing me a good morning and a happy Thanksgiving, asking if he can keep his shoes on. I've got a dirty apron on over my pajamas, NPR is airing an anthemic American something by the composer Aaron Copland, and two pecan pies are browning in the oven. The blue counter is a wall-to-wall mosaic of onions and celery and potatoes, boxes full of mushrooms, bags full of cranberries, bunches of parsley, thyme, and sage, bread waiting to be crumbed, and many sticks of butter earmarked for various dishes. *Plenty* is the word that pops into my head. We have plenty.

My dad thuds down onto the couch with a sigh, complains about how hot it is in the shack, even though yesterday morning he complained about the cold. It's like a Möbius strip of dissatisfaction—an impossible and never-ending paradox. When my dad finally freezes to death back there, he'll be fanning himself with a list of his grievances. I say I'll send Nick back to check on the thermostat, and he thanks me.

"The kids are sleeping?"

"The kids are sleeping."

"Sleeting?"

"No, no—just like you said, Dad. *Sleeping.*"

"It's sleeting," he says.

"What?"

"Sleeting?" He points to the glass door where I can see that it is, in fact, sleeting—a few wet clumps drifting down and melting on contact with the brown grass.

"Oh, yes, it's sleeting. And the kids are sleeping."

"Yes," he says. "Rocky, would you be so kind as to make me a cup of coffee?"

"I'd be delighted to, Dad," I say.

"Wait," he says. "I hadn't really looked at you. You are up to your elbows in a turkey's asshole. The coffee can wait."

Jamie, two and a half years old, once asked me to unwrap a string cheese while I was trying to fix the zipper on my jeans and then added, politely, "Whenever you're done looking at your penis, Mama." I promise my dad it will be only a minute, I'm just trying to figure out where they've hidden the neck and the giblets inside this enormous bird. "Aha!" I say and pull out a papery bag with dark shapes in it, which I tip out onto a paper towel. But the neck is somehow frozen to the inside the rib cage, and I can't peer into the cavity without feeling like the entire turkey is going to Mr. Bean its way onto my head.

"Yuck," I say, after a mist of turkey frost sprays my glasses. "It wasn't even supposed to be frozen to begin with."

"Maybe run some warm water on it?" my dad says, which is an excellent idea and works. I wash my glasses, make my dad's coffee and start heating butter in a pan to brown all these gruesome bits and bobs.

"Are you going to add a little wine to that?" my dad asks, and I say that I am.

"That's how Mom always did the gravy," he says, and I say that I know.

"Are you going to add a little tomato paste?" he asks, and I consider just saying yes but instead admit that I'm not.

"Mom always added a little tomato paste," he says, and I say that I know. "But you're not going to?" I'm not.

"I don't like doing the holidays without her. I mean any of the days, but maybe especially the holidays."

"I know, Dad," I say. "I feel the same way."

She used to do all the fiddly jobs I hate—cleaning the mushrooms and plucking parsley off of its stems, and just being so calm and lovely about all of it, a clean apron tied elegantly over the same black cashmere turtleneck she'd been wearing since the 1960s, when she wore it across the sea on the boat that landed her in New York. Any problem you ran into, she had a practical solution for it. You just needed to whisk in a teaspoon of cornstarch or a teaspoon of sugar or add a few cubes of raw potato. "No one will know the difference" was one of her reassuring mantras—usually when you were retrieving something you'd dropped onto the floor or scraping the burned part off of something else. She and my dad peeled potatoes together every year, sitting on the kitchen couch in their matching New Balance sneakers and competitively sloughing the peels right onto sheets of newspaper I'd laid out on the floor. How can she not be here? Grief is like the sound of the exhaust fan over the stove—a constant hum that recedes a little to the background over time, though you never get to turn it off.

"Why don't you use the name we gave you?" my dad says suddenly, aggrieved. "It's a beautiful name, Rachel."

I wipe my hands on my apron and turn from the stove to look at him. He's sipping his coffee argumentatively. "I do, Dad. I love the name Rachel. I use both."

"Was it your high school friends that started calling you Rocky?"

"Yeah," I say. "Ali, the rest of that friend group. Maybe junior high."

"Because of the guy who punched all that meat?"

I laugh. "Rocky Balboa. Yeah. I think they thought of me that way—kind of scrappy and fighty."

"I'm not a fan," he says, and I sigh, flip over the sizzling heart with a pair of tongs, say, "You never need to call me Rocky—although, I might add, you often choose to."

"Rachel was the name Mom chose for you," he says, and my eyes fill with tears.

"Dad, can you please not pick a random fight with me right now? There are a hundred people coming for dinner this afternoon. I'm really not in the mood."

"I'm sorry," he says. "I don't mean anything. I'm just being a shit-disturber for no reason."

"I'm sorry too, Dad," I say. "I'm just feeling kind of stressed and sensitive and sad." I pull the newspaper from its wrapper, fold it up, and hand it to him with a pen so he can do the crossword.

I'm back at the stove flipping the giblets around some more and sprinkling in the flour when he says, "*Erasable* pen."

"Yes, Dad. That's what I gave you."

"I thought you said *irascible* pen, which made a certain kind of sense."

I laugh, shake my head, tell him he's a pain but I love him.

"Do you need me to do something with Grandpa? Grandpa, are you getting in trouble with my mom?" Willa's awake, thank god!

"Good morning, Granddaughter," my dad says and then, sheepish, "I seem to be causing some disturbance, yes."

"I could hear you from upstairs," she says. "Do you need a little job to do? I'm talking to you the way my mom used to talk to us when we were bored and fighting. You could stand on the step stool and wash cranberries in the sink." My dad laughs.

"Speaking of," I say, and Willa says, "Even as I was saying that as a joke, I was hoping you were going to ask." Her staticky hair is sticking straight up. Talking to her is like trying to have a conversation with someone while they're being electrocuted.

Willa scrubs out the sink, fills it with cold water, and dumps in all five bags of cranberries. As a toddler, she used to stand here for hours in her galaxy-themed footie pajamas with a woolly pom-pom hat on, washing everything in sight—Tupperware, apples, silverware, LEGO—the water running and running. I can still hear her voice, which always had an edge of warning to it, because she was always a second away from losing her absolute mind about something or other. "I want to do washing at the sink," she would say, if she anticipated that you were about to try turning the faucet off—but the emphasis fell on the least expected words: "I WANT to do washing AT the SINK!" She was a tyrant masquerading as an elf, and you had to be very careful.

"Let's do a relish!" she says now. "With oranges and jalapeños." The berries float, a thick layer of garnet red, and she's swirling them around, plucking out any that look soft or puckered.

"No regular sauce?" my dad says, dejected, and Willa says, "No, no. Regular too. I'll do both."

"I think if I ate raw cranberries with a hot pepper in them my esophagus would fall out," my dad says, and Willa says, "Bestie. I got you." When I smile at him, he shrugs, mystified.

My dad, doing the Spelling Bee now, asks irritably why they allowed him *imply*. He says it like it rhymes with *pimply*. "I believe the correct word is *impish*," he says, and when I say *imPLY*, with a long y, he rolls his eyes at his own dementedness.

I'm taking the pies out of the oven when the door opens with a whoosh of cold air, and it's Nick, his hair soaked. "Oh!" I say. "I didn't realize you weren't here. Were you out for a run?"

He holds up the bag he's carrying. "Um, no, I wasn't out for a run. I was getting the heavy cream and ice you sent me out for, like, ten minutes ago."

"Oh god, thank you," I say. "I'm the worst." I kiss his cold cheek, whisk the gravy, unwrap a stick of butter, and turn back to the bird.

"Are you going to spatchcock it?" Nick asks, and I say no. He bends over it, moves the leg gently with his thumb and forefinger, watching. I don't even need to ask. This is just the physical therapist in him, I know, curious about joint articulation and the way muscle attaches to bone.

"Are you going to—what did Mom used to do? Wrap it in bandages? That can't be right," my dad says.

"I hope not," Willa says from the sink, where she's fishing out the bobbing cranberries with a strainer.

"Oh yeah, no," I say. "She used cheesecloth. I don't actually do it that way." I don't remind my dad that, even before my mom died, they'd been coming here for decades. The last bandaged turkey my mom roasted was probably sometime before the publication of *The Bridges of Madison County*.

Willa takes a picture of me smearing butter all over the big naked bird, and then Jamie and Maya pour into the kitchen like honey. I have to hug them with my elbows because my hands are now covered in salmonella.

"I woke up all excited about my Thanksgiving bagel," Jamie says, "but then I remembered that we don't have any leftovers yet." His day-after breakfast sandwich features stuffing, turkey, gravy, mashed potatoes, green beans, and cranberry sauce. Maya, his glossily gorgeous wife, makes a *poor baby* frownie face at me, and I laugh.

"There's actual lox," I say consolingly, and Jamie is consoled. He promises he'll do the sweet potatoes and mashed potatoes for me after breakfast.

"It already smells so good in here," he says—and it does. Sage and spices and the sugary brown smell of the pies.

They toast their bagels while I start crumbing bread in the food processor, apologizing for the noise and hoping we don't blow a fuse. Nick, meanwhile, is spraying the glass patio door with vinegar and smearing it around with newspaper. This—cleaning the one door and two bathroom mirrors—is something I asked if he would do before Thanksgiving, which today no longer is.

I stop the food processor. "Honey," I say. "I'm sorry, but that's really smeary."

"You're probably seeing the other side," he says mildly, "which I haven't done yet."

"I'm definitely not," I say. "It's definitely this side. Hey, you can't just use the same single piece of sodden newspaper to do every glass surface in the house."

"I'm not," he says. "It's fine. I'm on it." I don't know what a gorge is or means, but I can feel mine rising. Sweat breaks out along my hairline, and I wouldn't be surprised to see video footage of steam curling out of my ears. Ho, hey, menopause is in the house! Everyone has gone silent and the toaster dings.

"Don't gaslight me," I say, and Willa says, "Mama, can you not pick a fight with Dad on Thanksgiving?"

"Yes," I answer her, sixteen seconds later, because I have been breathing in through my nose for a count of three, holding it for six, and breathing out for seven. *Breathe in gratitude*, I think to myself, snidely—except I really am so lucky and I know it. "Sorry, everyone! Just being a bitch as per holiday tradition." I am furious and also want the day to be nice. Nick is the best and also the worst. What I should have done, I'm thinking transactionally, is blown him in the shower this morning—to bake a little flexibility and forgiveness into the day ahead. Plus it would have given me longer to deep-condition my hair. But that opportunity has come and gone.

I ask Maya about her work at the museum, and she stands near me with her toasted honey-butter bagel chatting about sea creatures while I chop mushrooms and onions for the stuffing. Jamie and my dad are on the couch, drinking coffee and showing each other their investments—it's probably all Lockheed Martin or prison uniforms. Willa is at the stove now, measuring sugar and spices into the pot of cranberries. She's switched out my music and put on an excellent playlist in which every song is about depressed girls having raucous sex with each other. I remind her to set some cranberry sauce aside for the cream cheese pie.

"Rocky, sorry—I know this isn't the time probably," Maya says quietly, leaning toward me so I can hear her over the music. She pushes her darkly shining hair behind her ears, then pulls the sleeves of her pink flannel pajamas over her hands. "But try to go easy on Jamie, okay? I mean, I know you are. But he's having a harder time with everything than you might think."

"Oh," I say quietly. "Am I being hard on Jamie?" I ask, instead of saying, *My son, who I've known since before he was born?* I scrape all the veggies from the cutting board into a huge bowl to make more room for chopping. I have never in my life felt like more of a mother-in-law.

"I don't know," she says. "I mean, I'm sure you're not. But I think he feels like you're mad at him. Like the thing you said about health insurance at dinner last night."

I had been complaining about the way my insurance company will put you on hold indefinitely when you call to check on your claims, and then they make you punch in your ninety-digit ID number so they can put you on hold again, and then they say it's not covered—whatever it is, even if it was getting your own chopped-off head stapled back on—because you picked an out-of-plan provider or it was an unapproved procedure or it involved an off-label use of some or other drug.

In the middle of all of it, they ask for the answer to your two-factor authentication, even though they won't tell you what the question is, so you're just guessing your first pet, your mother's maiden name, the city you were born in, your day swallowed up by personal trivia until you happen to stumble on the right answer, which is the name of your favorite team—the New York Giants, apparently—even though you hate sports in general and football in particular. Every denial has to be appealed, every medication has to be resubmitted for coverage, the deductible is never met and recedes into the infinite future because it's all a fun house of financial ruin. I will be dead in my casket with the phone pressed to my cold ear, on hold about the copay for my vaginal estrogen.

"Ah," I say. "That wasn't specific to Jamie."

"Hm," Maya says. "You did mention Dickens by name." Oh, shit, did I? I did! I'd read somewhere that Dickens basically invented the way insurance companies work, with the famous strategic trifecta of *Delay, Deny, Destroy*. Or maybe that last one is *Derange*? I couldn't quite remember. *Decompose? Dement?* The thing that makes you give up and just pay the bill yourself because they have fully broken you and sapped you of the will to live. Or the thing that, more famously, might make you literally homicidal. Every insurance company practices it now, apparently. Jamie didn't seem to know quite what I was talking about, although he said, "Yeah, that tracks," about Dickens being involved.

"I didn't mean to implicate Jamie, exactly," I say, but I can feel that this isn't quite accurate.

Maya nods noncommittally. "I'm sorry, Rocky. Butting in

is not really my comfort zone." This seems inarguably true. She is the least meddlesome person I know. Whatever the opposite of a drama queen is, that's what she is. A chill king. "But maybe you want to check in with him. I know he doesn't want to give you something else to worry about today, but it would probably be good to clear the air."

"Thank you," I say. "I truly appreciate the heads-up." To prove this, I put my knife down so that I can smile at her without a knife in my hand, and she smiles back.

"What can I do to help?" she says, but maybe my feelings are a little bit hurt, because I hear myself say, "I don't think anything. I think we're good here." Willa, behind me at the stove, sighs audibly.

Chapter 31

The turkey is sizzling in the oven, the stuffing is ready to bake, the pies are cooling on a rack, the cranberry sauces are made, there's a fire in the woodstove, and Willa and Maya are cutting up carrots and celery for dipping. "Don't forget the radishes!" I say, and Willa waves me away with her hand. Nick is looking in the basement for the gravy boats and the fat separator; when I go down to check on him, he's evaluating an assortment of things he's laid out on the warped Ping-Pong table: the fondue set, a box of old mason-jar lids, a collection of enormous plastic theme-park cups with plastic accordion straws. "Oh god, honey!" I say, and he tells me it's fine. I find Jamie in the living room with my dad and ask if he wants to walk outside with me.

"Of course," he says cheerfully. "Sleet is one of my favorite forms of precipitation."

"I do know that about you," I say. "After snow and mist, but before hail and freezing rain."

"Exactly," he says.

"I'd come with you," my dad says, "but I don't really want to."

"Fair," I say. "If I set up the whetstone in the kitchen, will you sharpen my knives for me?"

"I'd be delighted," he says. "Five minutes. I can't really get up right now." He gestures to Angie, asleep in his lap, all her limbs tucked under her like she's a baked potato.

"Anytime would be great," I say. "Just the chef's knife and the paring knife. Don't bother with the randoms. The knife stepchildren can just relax and be dull."

Outside the sleet has stopped. There's a low shelf of dark clouds, but still the sky feels deliciously high and vast. We can smell the wet leaves, the smoke from everybody's woodstove. "Oh!" I say. "I thought I was grumpy in there, but maybe I was just claustrophobic." Jamie alleges to know what I mean, although *grumpy* is not really part of his mood repertoire.

We head into the woods and all the tree trunks are wetly black, patches of lichen glowing a faint blue-green against the dark bark. "I'm sorry, honey," I say, and he says, "Me too."

"What for?" I ask.

He jumps up to touch a high branch. "Disappointing you, I guess."

I stop walking, horrified. "Disappointing me? Are you kidding?"

He stops walking too and looks directly at me, flecks of gold and green glittering in the brown of his eyes. "I mean, obviously I know you love me," he says and smiles. "But I'm not kidding, no."

"I'm not disappointed by you," I say. "My god, honey. Never." He tips his head side to side—*Maybe, maybe not.*

"But do you want me to feel bad, Mama? I feel like you kind of want me to feel worse than I do."

"That can't be true," I say, as if I'm talking about some unknowable thing other than myself. But it might be true. If he felt worse than he seems to, I'd want him to feel better. I've been trying to prove to myself that Miles Zapf's death isn't his fault—even as I want to make sure he understands that it might be. "I feel like he's already completely forgiven himself," I complained to Nick last night, and Nick said, "People make mistakes." "I don't think greed is a mistake, exactly," I said. I didn't mean our son, really—I just meant the whole consulting enterprise, I guess. "Besides forgiving himself," Nick said, "what other choice does Jamie have?" This was a hard concept for me to process. *Permanent guilt and misery*, I didn't say, given that I recognize this as an unwholesome approach to life. I would never want Jamie to feel the way I do.

"And I already feel worse than you might imagine," Jamie says.

"Oh, honey," I say. *I might be dying of a weird liver disease*, I think, out of the blue—although it is always there, that drumbeat of fear. *How will I have wanted to spend this time?*

"Yeah. I mean, even if I didn't go to high school with him it would be awful. But this way it's like the kind of movie where we could have switched places." I don't totally know what he means, but I get the flavor of it—two interchangeable young lives.

"That sounds like a bad way to feel," I say, and he says, "Cat hair," and reaches out his delicate fingers to pull something from my eyelashes. I'm smiling at him—beaming, even under these circumstances—and thinking of a trip we took to Jamaica, just a few years ago. At the bar where Jamie and I were waiting for our rum punches and chargrilled clams, a local pointed to Jamie and said to me, "You should take him to the donkey races—it's lots of fun for kids." "Thanks," I'd said. Jamie and I were laughing. "I mean, he's twenty-five—but thanks!" "Oh," he'd said. "The way you look at him. I thought he was much younger." Now Jamie just says *donkey races* to me whenever I dote. He doesn't say it now, though.

"Even the accident aside," Jamie says. "I mean, you already hate that I work there."

"Ugh," I say, because he's right.

I used to talk to Nick and the kids when I was writing my etiquette column—I'd read aloud the dilemmas and we'd discuss our thoughts. The questions were all over the place. What do I do about my neighbor's unbearable wind chimes, my mother-in-law's suffocating myrrh body wash, my cousin who comes to the dinner table in a string bikini, the friends who named their twin sons Claude Monet and Vincent van Gogh? But every individual question was really a version of the same existential one: *People are different from me. How do I survive it?*

"With as much grace as possible" was our answer, every time. What else is there?

My son works for a management consulting firm that's hurting people. What do I do?

If you're not careful, you'll end up mistaking difference for loss—which is how you lose everything.

"I'm so sorry, honey," I say, and Jamie nods.

"I haven't drunk the Kool-Aid, Mama," he says. "I don't

believe that we have no moral responsibility to people in the world."

"I know," I say.

"Odds are tricky. Sometimes the outcome is bad, even if the risk was vanishingly small."

WHEN I WAS PREGNANT WITH Jamie, Nick and I took a class at the hospital about babyproofing our house. The teacher told a story about a toddler pulling herself up on the handle of the oven door, and the oven toppling over and crushing her. "So, should we secure the oven to the wall?" I asked, terrified, and she said no, no. It was really just an example of the kind of random tragedy that could happen to anyone. Jamie and Willa's driver's ed teacher told them about a local driver getting shot and killed at a red light by a person with a crossbow. "Not ten miles from here!" she'd said, excited. "What do I do with that?" Willa asked me, furious and alarmed. "How does that knowledge help me make safe driving decisions?"

"A LOW PROBABILITY OF A bad thing happening doesn't mean it can't or won't," Jamie says.

"I understand," I say. "Only one in one hundred thousand people are diagnosed with primary sclerosing cholangitis every year. But that one person has to be *somebody*."

"We got a memo from the CEO," he says. "After the accident. It was basically, like, *Your assessments were correct, good job, it's nobody's fault.*"

"You didn't love that," I say, and he says, "I didn't."

I want to ask if he's reconsidering the value of the work, but that's not the right question and I know it. Miles Zapf's mom, Christine, must have had a last conversation with her son, even though she wouldn't have known that's what it was. Did she feel so lucky, just to be talking to him, her living child? What did she say? What did she stop herself from saying?

I feel so grateful to be getting to talk to you is what I'm thinking. I say it out loud, and Jamie smiles at me. "We're different, and I love you so much, honey." You have to forgive everyone, whether or not they ask for forgiveness.

"I like money," Jamie says, and slings a long arm over my shoulders. Sweet child of mine.

"I know you do," I say. I'm remembering the voice-operated safe he had as a child, where he stashed all the cash anyone ever gave him. The code word was *pencil*, but Jamie pronounced it *penis hole* to make Willa laugh. "Penis hole!" you'd hear him yelling in his room. "Penis hole!" It meant he'd be in there counting his money like a joyful miser.

"I like lamb," he says. "So sue me."

"Shit," I say. "The turkey." So we turn around and head for home, where I will haul the bird from the oven and my dad will watch me carve it while our guests arrive with more pie, dinner rolls, beautiful cheese, bottles of gorgeous wine I won't drink, and flowers Angie will secretly eat and conspicuously throw up. We'll have hot cider, Jamie's mashed potatoes and sweet potatoes, Willa's cranberries two ways. Oniony stuffing with butter-crisped edges. Buttered green beans and roasted Brussels sprouts and a green salad I'll forget to serve. Maya will sit next to me at the long table, and that will feel like forgiveness. Then we'll tumble out into the darkness—all of us, even my dad—to walk down the street under the starlit glow of our own gratitude, to walk back to the beckoning amber of our windowpanes and hope that with all of that walking and thanksgiving we'll have made enough room for pie.

Chapter 32

On Miles Zapf's last night on Earth, he would have arrived at the Masonic lodge while the musicians were warming up their instruments: banjo, guitar, cello, accordion, recorder, kick drum. The music was already beginning to circle the room, gathering people up and stitching them together like an invisible needle and thread. The floor was vibrating—electric with anticipation. *Hello, hello!* He was hugged half to death by a dozen people. *Miles!* He took in the rainbow of swirling skirts worn by people of all genders. Purple shirts and purple shawls. Hand-knit socks and bare feet. Long hair and crew cuts and beards and kilts. Teenagers and old people and babies in backpacks. Sharpies were passed around so everyone could fill out a name tag: Mark, Sarah, Wren, Habib, Athena. Sixty others. *Miles.* At some point the caller would have started organizing the dancers. It was a summer evening—eight o'clock sunshine streaming through the windows—and she said to them, "We're dancing in community. We're in this together. If someone needs help, help them." Everyone whooped and clapped.

Or so I imagine. Because that's what she says to us now, although it's a dark December night and the space is illuminated only by fluorescent strip lighting. It's warm nonetheless. Aglow.

Everyone whoops and claps. "We want to learn this first dance in honor of our own Miles Zapf," the caller says. "Who we cherish and miss." People snap and clap and call out their affirmations. This is why I'm here—because of Miles. Christine had posted the event on Facebook. *Beginners welcome!* the description noted. But what about the morbidly curious? Are we welcome too? My eyes are on the names around me, although if Christine is in the room, I haven't spotted her. "If you're new here, you're in luck," the caller says. "Because nobody else knows this dance yet either!" Everybody laughs. She ushers us into a big circle, instructs us to hold hands, to make eye contact with our neighbors, right and left. To have fun. Some people are still weeping, still wiping their faces with their sleeves or handkerchiefs, but then they extend their fingers. All of us are masked. "We need to keep our immunocompromised family safe," the caller reminds us, and I think, blandly, *How nice*, and then realize: *Oh—that's* me*!* and feel a jolt of gratitude. I raise my hand shyly when the new dancers are asked to identify themselves. "Welcome," she says. "All of you—give yourselves the grace to make mistakes. Give it to each other too. And for fuck's sake," she adds, "have fun!" Everybody laughs again.

 She talks us through the basics: the balance and swing, the allemande and do-si-do. We're shuffled into roles—robins and larks—and suddenly we're moving up the hall and down the hall, and already I am laughing, my glasses fogging up. And then the music starts. We're in pairs and foursomes, passed from person to person, twirled and spun and paraded around, stopping every now and then to stomp on the beat, which is my favorite part. It's like we're in a drunken, churning Irish dance hall, although it's a substance-free event. It's like we're in a choreographed Merchant Ivory ball scene, although some people are wearing what appear to be lumpily homemade shoes. There are hands on my waist and shoulders, hands in my hands, eyes locked on mine, it is dizzying and chaotic and I'm laughing so much I can barely catch my breath. The music swells and speeds up and we're spinning past each other—it's a hey, apparently—and we're weaving through each other, grouping and regrouping and making some kind of tapestry of everything we are, which is love in motion.

I don't know that Miles would have laughed the whole entire time, especially given that nobody else seems to be doing that but me. And yeah, sure, there's a mean old white lady here—like a stock character from central casting called The Mean Old White Lady. "No," she calls to me, whenever I stagger past her, laughing. "No. This way. Ugh! To the left! No!" But it's just her. Everybody else is the opposite of *no*. We're the *yes, and* of improv and, as instructed, we are pure grace, given and received. Also, I am peeing in my pants a little bit.

I leave between sets, and I'm not even sure why. I'm just overwhelmed and overflowing and I want to come back and dance again when I don't feel like a detective. Or a spy. Also, it's late and I'm tired. I tumble outside and lean against the door with a hand on my heart, like a girl who's been kissed at the end of a perfect date. It's oddly bright out, and at first I don't understand why—but it's because of the snow! It's snowing. There's already half an inch on the ground, and more is drifting down in flakes and clumps. I can see it beneath the old-fashioned streetlamp. I head for home beneath the avenue of massive oak trees, my heart pounding inside my living body. There's an ache beneath my ribs, and it's not exactly new, but I don't know what it is.

"THERE AREN'T PAIN RECEPTORS IN the liver itself," the Boston hepatologist explained to me, palpating my abdomen gently. "But this kind of dull ache in the surrounding tissue might be caused by inflammation," he said. There was a Harvard medical student sitting in on the appointment, and when I looked at him, he shrugged a little nervously.

"Harvard!" I said. "Are your parents so proud?"

His shiny cheeks pinkened, and he laughed and nodded. "Oh my god, yes!" he said. "Although they tell everyone I'm doing a rotation in *herpetology*, and I can't bring myself to tell them that's snakes."

Sometimes on an airplane, at takeoff, I look at the strangers sitting next to me and wonder if they're about to become a significant part of my life—like if the plane gets hijacked or drops suddenly into the Atlantic with a splash. Will I experience the end of it all with these people I've only ever shared an armrest with? I felt that here, about these two, although I realized that this was not that kind of disaster.

"We brought your imaging to our monthly special cases meeting," the doctor said. He was holding my shin in his hands, tracing the rash, which had started to recede like a horrible, lumpy tide finally going back out to sea.

"Yikes!" I said. "I like to be special, but not in this exact way."

The doctor smiled indulgently. "I wanted to see if anybody had thoughts about how these lesions might concur with the liver findings," he said. "Occam's razor—we like to find the simplest explanation. It seems highly unlikely that you would have two rare, unrelated diseases."

"And?" I said. The word *disease* still took me aback. I mean, just being human is a terminal condition, sure—but *disease* kind of runs a highlighter pen over it. Also *lesions* is not my favorite.

He shrugged. "Sarcoidosis could explain both?" he said. "But then, nobody really liked it as an explanation for either. I think we don't really know what the connection might be."

"Are disease names just metaphors?" I said. It had started to seem so much less scientific to me than what I'd always imagined. Diagnosis was more like decorators holding up a paint swatch and eyeballing a match than like researchers squinting through a microscope and making objective determinations.

"Hm," he said. "That's not how we think of them. But sometimes, yes, it's a little like the umbrella that we can gather the most symptoms beneath."

"I feel well," I said defensively, and he said, "That's good! That's great."

"The blood work is almost normal," the med student added. "I mean, your liver is basically crushing it."

The game Chutes and Ladders really does prepare you for life, doesn't it? The constant ascending and descending—every good and bad thing seeming, in moments, so random and temporary. Eat too many unripe apples and get a bile duct stricture.

"We're sticking with primary sclerosing cholangitis as a provisional diagnosis," the doctor said.

"Ugh," I said. Magical thinking had led me astray yet again!

I'd pictured a scenario where it all turned out to be a misunderstanding or maybe the radiologist just needed new glasses or was drunk. "Don't be surprised when I send you a holiday ham or do some other weird thing to brownnose my way to the top of the transplant list," I said. I was relieved not to hear the words *blow job* come out of my mouth.

The doctor laughed. "No need," he said. "You're just at the very earliest stages of this disease. Or you have a very mild case of it. Or both. We'll keep an eye on you. PSC increases your risk of certain cancers, so we'll screen you every six months. There are some promising medications in the pipeline, Rachel. So even if it progresses, there might be treatment available in the future."

"Yikes," I said, and he said, "A little bit of yikes. You can visit with the fear, but don't hire a van and move there."

"That's really good advice," I said, and he smiled and snapped his iPad shut, and the two of them said good-bye and left me to change.

NOW I AM WALKING HOME under the trees, the snow falling bright and steady through the gaps, the ache throbbing a little with my heartbeat. Miles Zapf left that thrumming ecstasy of dancers and then his car was hit by a train. I'm as alive as I've ever been and somebody's child is dead, and an owl hoots from the tippy-top of a white pine like it's answering a question I haven't even thought to ask.

Chapter 33

Here I am, on shore, dread-filled and resolute, zipped into neoprene booties and tugging neoprene gloves onto my fingers. It's New Year's Day. Nick and I are at a local reservoir with a group of fifty or so people, all of us preparing to dip into the hole we've chipped from the ice with axes and shovels and a kettlebell on a rope. This is our fifth time polar-plunging since the weekend after Thanksgiving, and I am wildly in love.

A friend of mine had recommended an isolation tank as a way to regulate my immune system—she even gave me a gift certificate—but I never went. This was the same friend who boasted that she didn't take any medications and hated the idea of them. *That's weird—I* love *taking medications!* I thought of saying, but I was too weary for sass. And then I'd felt so despondent even just imagining the experience she was offering me. My body is already too much like an isolation tank: lonely, private, confining. What I really need is this: the rowdy crowds of people stripping down on the beach to their swimsuits and wool hats like lunatic penguins in an animated film.

"I've got a horrible rash!" I announced the first time we went. "Okay," they said. "Brace yourselves!" I cried, peeling out of my down jacket and flannel bathrobe. "It's not contagious, but it's gnarly." Everybody nodded, laughed, admired the rash when it came to light. And that was that. I'm learning to detach my mind from fear. I stand at the water's edge and I pull the plug on catastrophic chatter—*You will die!*—so that I can wade into the full, glorious crazy. I slice through the water like a knife's blade, and the water is a knife's blade, slicing me back, and I am quiet and determined.

Even gloved, our delicate, bony fingers are vulnerable to the cold, and so we all hold our hands up out of the water, fingers tented, as if in prayer. And it's a kind of frigid baptism, but I'm not praying, not really, although if I *were* praying I would probably just pray for this. Maybe this and everyone I love staying well and safe forever and me living to see it. Just that one measly little wish, ha ha ha.

I MET WITH AN ACUPUNCTURIST last week, showed her the rash, tried to explain the way it might or might not be related to this liver disease that I might or might not have and that might or might not kill me. She listened, nodded, and saw through me. "Are you sleeping?" she asked, and I said no, not really. I surprised myself by telling her about Miles Zapf, about Jamie, and also about my pounding fear of death—my own and everyone else's. "But why do you feel like your life has swerved off course?" she asked, quoting myself back to me. I knew she'd been listening closely, so I didn't repeat my story—I just shook my head. "I mean, why isn't this just your life's proper course?" she said.

"Because it's painful and scary?" I said, and she moved to embrace me as I cried. She smelled of woodsmoke and oranges.

Later, she inserted tiny whiskers of needles all over me—my

scalp and wrists and hands and feet—and when she tapped one gently into my abdomen I cried out. "Oh, you're feeling that one!" she said, excited, and I said yes, that it hurt. "Are you sure it's pain?" she said, and I said I wasn't. "That's your liver," she explained. "That particular point? It's called the Gate of Hope." The Gate of Hope! "And maybe that sensation isn't pain," she said to me then, using a tissue to wipe the tears that were pooling in my hair. "Maybe what you're feeling is your life. It's the full, expansive possibility of being alive." And maybe it was.

I went home and slept deeply, and when I woke up, my dad was already sitting in the kitchen, neatly dressed and ready for the day. *If he can survive the loss of my mom*, I thought, *then I can survive anything.* Can I, though? After I sat down next to him, both of us holding steaming cups of coffee topped up with eggnog, he cleared his throat. "What?" I said. "Do you need to be Heimliched or are you about to tell me something bad?"

"Neither, I don't think," he said. Next to him, the woodstove hissed and crackled, and beyond that our Christmas tree glittered with lights and angels and various lumpy salt-dough shapes from the children's childhoods, and also, perversely, a blown-glass menorah topper. I had done a great job with the kids' stockings—filled them with high-end body wash and wool socks and German chocolate. "Rachel, as you know, I've kept the apartment all this time."

"Yes," I said. We still stayed there occasionally when we drove him down for doctor's appointments or to visit Jamie and Maya. Letting it go would be sad, of course. I grew up there, for one thing. And for another, we'd be forced finally to sort through my mother's letters and clothing and her enormous hatbox full of embroidery thread. My eyes welled with tears just imagining it—everything looking and smelling so precisely of her. Her elegant handwriting; her neatly folded sweaters; her delicate perfume with its notes of jasmine and rose. I could already feel that this was going to be a test of my endurance, grief-wise. Also stuff-wise. How much would my dad hope to bring back to the house? Maybe we could rent a storage unit and put everything in purgatory while he figured out what he wanted to keep.

"Wait, what?" I said. I hadn't actually been listening.

"I was saying that I'm going to go back after the new year. It's been lovely here with you, but it's time to move on."

"Time to move on?" *You're almost ninety-three years old!* I didn't say. *You can't just free-bird back to the big city!* But he could, of course, and planned to. "Willa's moving out too," I didn't add, because I didn't want to be tragic—but it was true. She and Sunny were looking for an apartment in town. "Who will make your coffee?" I said, petulantly, instead.

My dad sighed. "I can make my own coffee, believe it or not. I probably won't be able to live alone for long, but for a little longer I want to. It was too hard right after we lost Mom, but now I can try. I can always order in takeout or groceries."

"Yes," I said. My eyes were brimming now, and I tipped my head back a little to force the tears back into those tiny corner holes they'd come from. "You don't think something like assisted living would be a more appropriate next step?"

Appropriate had been his own standard for everything when I was a teenager, and I winced to hear it boomerang back at him.

"I just want to try on my own for a little while," he said again. "I wasn't quite done with the part of my life where I wasn't just a lumpy dependent."

"That's not what you are," I said, and he sighed.

"I honestly thought you'd be relieved."

"Well, I'm not," I said. "Does that change anything?"

"No," he said, and smiled. "I'll be back before you know it." These would be less rosy circumstances; we both understood this fact and traded exaggerated grimaces. "And I can always call Jamie if I need anything." This was accurate. "One thing I love about Jamie," my mom had said once, "is that whenever you call him he answers his phone." This was so wholly untrue about Jamie as a rule that the information stunned me. "He's a good child" was all I could say back.

"I'll miss you, though," my father said now.

"I'll miss you too, Dad." The lump in my throat was part sorrow and part gratitude. Maybe that's what it always is, and we just forget to notice how lucky we are because we're so busy choking and trying not to cry. *But what if he dies?* I thought. *Or I do?* And what if I never know anything certain again for the rest of my life? "Except love," someone said. "You know that for sure." And that someone was, of course, me.

"Except love," my dad said back to me, laughing and confused, because apparently I'd said this out loud.

"Except love," I said again, and the cats jumped into our laps and we turned our big ship of a conversation around to talk about the weather. A blizzard was in the forecast, and I was going to need to salt the driveway.

AFTER A COUPLE OF ROUNDS of acupuncture, I started sleeping more regularly. I'd still wake in the night and poke around to read scientific papers about liver disease or to see what Christine Zapf was posting on Facebook: It looked like she was settling with the railroad company; it looked like she celebrated Christmas with family. One night I sent Jamie a Buy Nothing screenshot—somebody was gifting an oil painting of Mrs. Doubtfire—and he hearted it immediately. *You're up!* I wrote. *Why are you up at four in the morning?* Three dots, then nothing, then a cry-laughing emoji. *Everything okay?* I wrote. *You need anything?* I've always been as appalled by the book *The Giving Tree* as the next person. The myth that mothers exist just to get all our apples tugged off before being sawn apart limb by limb? It's grotesque, of course. But what wouldn't we give our children, if we could? What wouldn't we sacrifice? If it would bring Jamie solace, he'd be welcome to anything I have or am. Willa too. Take it! Take it all! Grind down the rotten stump if it's in your way! Sorry if my martyrdom gives you the ick! Three dots appeared. *No, I'm good,* he wrote. *I got a job offer from Rockefeller. Philanthropic consulting. Less money, but good money. It looks interesting.*

Wow! I wrote. I made no snide comments about ruthless philanthropic billionaires. *Sounds great, honey,* I wrote, and it honestly did. *Congratulations on getting the offer, whatever you decide to do.*

Thanks, he said. *We'll see. Try to sleep, Mama, okay? You too,* I wrote. Then powered off my phone and curled up to Nick's warm back.

HERE IN THE FREEZING WATER now, my brain is rewarding me with neurochemicals. Endorphins and dopamine and maybe, because this is a love affair, oxytocin too. Everyone is so beautiful! I am flooded with pleasure. If someone said, *Let's stay in until we freeze to death!* I'd probably say, *Okay!* If we were doing this in the dark, we would see each other's teeth gleaming in the moonlight, behind our massive smiles. Give me solace, but make it burn with cold.

Back in our Subaru, Nick and I will blast the heat and warm up again, like our bodies are engines designed to do exactly this, because they are. Life is a near-death experience. And death is a real-life one. There is—as I stubbornly wrote in that piece I finally submitted—only this, now. One day, will we look back and think: *Wow, that was a hard year?* Will we be damaged and scarred, but okay? Or will we think: *That was when things first started to get bad?*

There's no telling. Only this—loving each other like there's plenty of room on the life raft. Like there's no tomorrow—or like there is one, and you don't want to wake up hungover with regret. You just want to wake up while you still can. While the world is turning and the owls are calling and gratitude is the very air you are still breathing, because, whatever happens next, that's how lucky you are.

You are still breathing.

Acknowledgments

Sara Nelson keeps saying *yes* to me, which is everything; I love getting to say the words *my editor*. Is it weird to mention that the HarperCollins team is starting to feel like family? Do they worry I'll show up at the holidays with a casserole? Too bad! I might! Maya Baran and Katie O'Callaghan are almost mystically excellent at their jobs and are also so much fun to know. Diana Velasquez makes it all happen and makes me feel like less of a freak, which is no small task. Edie Astley brings her graciousness and intelligence to every book. Tina Andreadis and Emi Battaglia have stepped in and stepped up so cheerfully that I am shaking my head in wonder and gratitude. Deliciously meticulous copy editor Janet Rosenberg fills my family group chat with her excellent style-sheet entries (Coily: tiny spring from a pen; Angie's companion). And library geniuses Virginia Stanley, Grace Caternolo, and Lainey Mays are so full of joy that they inspire me even beyond the world of publishing.

And somehow I get to keep having my same wonderful Doubleday team in the UK, including: my editor Kirsty Dunseath, who is a fantastic reader as well as a funny and deeply caring person; my astonishingly talented publicist and traveling partner Alison Barrow; creative-genius cover designer Beci Kelly. Plus so many other amazing people, including Queen Rih, Emily Harvey, Phoebe Llanwarne, the PRH export team, and Georgie Bewes.

My agent Jennifer Gates keeps being here with me, with her kindness and her brilliance. Thank you, also, to the rest of the Aevitas folks, including Allison Warren, Erin Files, Vanessa Kerr, and Mags Chmielarczyk, who keep enthusiastically foisting my books on unsuspecting filmmakers and countries.

Thank you, beloved readers—from the casual page leafers to the devoted bookstagammers—for reading the books, buying the books, requesting the books at your library and checking them out and reviewing them. Thank you to all the beloved librarians, booksellers, indie bookstores, book reviewers, blurbers, book clubs, festival organizers, podcasters, interviewers, and listeners. Thank you for hosting me, for hand-selling the book, for allowing me to make a living as a writer. Thank you, Ann Patchett, for decades of reading bliss, for the blurb that launched a metaphorical thousand reprints, and for being such a champion in every way. Thank you Elin Hildebrand and Tim Ehrenberg for your Nantucket magic.

Special thanks to Michael Millner for allowing me to make you read stand-alone chapters suddenly and out of order, and for laughing at my jokes; to Birdy Newman for editing the manuscript with your huge heart and enormous discernment; to Ben Newman for talking so patiently and imaginatively with me about what might have happened and how Jamie might have felt about it. Thanks to Snapper and Jellyfish for providing constant comfort and excellent source material on cats and how they behave.

A few very specific thank-yous: to Jane Yolen and John Schoenherr for *Owl Moon*; to Walt Bogdanich and Michael Forsythe for *When McKinsey Comes to Town*; to Nicholas Faith for *Derail: Why Trains Crash*; to Jill Kaufman for her thoughts on *As the World Turns*; to Analua Moreira for both the Cracker Barrel deflection and Weird Al's daughter; to Katharine Whittemore for *organ recital*; to Madeleine DelVicario's cousin Frieda for her dot-tastic feeling; to Maddie herself for so many things, including being stoned on the way to the campground bathroom and mistaking me for Wee Willie Winkie (I'm sorry I skipped the part about the turd that turned out to be a donut hole); to Alyson Millner for *when you're done looking at your penis*; to Birdy Newman and Illia Kawash-Cooper for real-life suture removal; to Kannan Jagannathan for being the physicist friend; to doctors Sotonye Imadojemu, Danielle O'Banion, Daniel Pratt, Laura Tarter, and Stephen Zucker for the obvious reasons; to Margie Kolchin for the Gate of Hope; to Joanna Goddard for many things, but especially for letting me write about polar-plunging; to Amherst Contra Dance for allowing Rocky and me to imagine what Miles Zapf might have experienced during his last night on Earth.

Thank you to the Rowland Writers Retreat, both the generous founders and the incredible friends I made there. I completed these final edits on the shores of Lake Cayuga.

Ohhhh, and all the usual, beautiful suspects: my mom friends, Wednesday tennis friends, Amherst College friends, hospice friends, weird friends, writing friends, work friends, polar-plunge Coldies, online friends, young-people friends, and my oldest friends in the world, here and gone. You all know who you are. Special shout-outs to: the Amherst Tire Running Club (Kathleen Traphagen and Becky Michaels); my sickness-and-health Maddie DelVicario; Lydia Elison, who scrubs my brain out while I'm just trying to do a single measly push-up; and to the rest of my forever tribe: Gordon Bigelow, Lee Bowie, Andrew Coburn, Khalid Elkalai, Judy Frank, Judy Haas, Ann Hallock, Jen Jarrell, Sam Marion, Meredith Michaels, Rebecca Morgan, Jeremy Pomeroy, Jennifer Rosner, the Shahmehri-Costellos, Laura Tisdel, Emily Todd, the entire VanTaylor-Pomeroy group, and Cornelius Walker.

Thank you to my brother, Robert Newman, for being so fully in all of it with me. Thank you to my niblings and cousins and aunts and uncles, and also my many, many in-laws, including and especially Larry Millner and Julia Hunter.

My parents, Ted and Jennifer Newman, have been forced to experience a kind of annoying shadow life as Rocky's parents, even though they're so much better than the fictional versions. They're the very best. My beautiful mother, for example, is very much alive and makes excellent coffee. "Are you ever going to write about the fact that I had an important job at a major corporation?" my dad asked recently, and, sadly, no, I'm not. And even though you think I make you sound like a half-sour pickle salesman or a mobster from Murder, Incorporated, at least I gave you all the funniest lines (again).

Oh, Michael Millner, how I adore you! You make everything possible, and I know it's not always—or even usually—easy.

Thank you for your steadiness and hotness and laughter and caretaking, and for reading *Amos and Boris* to me, from memory, during so many of the darkest nights.

Ben and Birdy Newman: Loves of my life. Thank you for being so patient and real, so loving and fun and funny. I am the luckiest, and I know it.

About the Author

CATHERINE NEWMAN has written numerous columns, articles, and canned-bean recipes for magazines and newspapers, and her essays have been widely anthologized. She is the author of the novels *Sandwich*, which was an instant *New York Times* bestseller, and *We All Want Impossible Things*; the memoirs *Waiting for Birdy* and *Catastrophic Happiness*; the middle-grade novel *One Mixed-Up Night*; and the bestselling kids' life-skills books *How to Be a Person* and *What Can I Say?* She lives in Amherst, Massachusetts.

Find Catherine at cronesandwich.substack.com.